Breaking Trail

Breaking Trail

JOANNE BELL

GROUNDWOOD BOOKS
HOUSE OF ANANSI PRESS
TORONTO BERKELEY

Groundwood Books / House of Anansi Press
110 Spadina Avenue, Suite 801, Toronto, ON M5V 2K4

Distributed in the USA by Publishers Group West
1700 Fourth Street, Berkeley, CA 94710

We acknowledge for their financial support of our publishing program the Canada Council for the Arts, the Government of Canada through the Book Publishing Industry Development Program (BPIDP) and the Ontario Arts Council.

Library and Archives Canada Cataloging in Publication
Bell, Joanne.
Breaking Trail / Joanne Bell.
ISBN 0-88899-630-6 (bound). — ISBN 0-88899-662-4 (pbk.)
I.Title.
PS8603.E52B74 2005 jC813'.6 C2004-906453-3

Cover illustration by Julia Bell

Printed and bound in Canada

For Elizabeth

Acknowledgments

Thanks to Mary, Ren and Elizabeth for reading my stories, Alex W. for helping with the dogs, and the members of the Dawson Young Author's Club for years of writing enthusiasm.

Thanks especially to my father for encouraging me to hurry up, and my mother for passing along her love of what's beautiful.

Finally, thanks to Mikin for being Mikin.

Prologue

BEAR'S HEAD almost touches the cab roof of Dad's pickup. I kiss his nose and bury my face in his black fur.

"I'm going to find dogs as smart and friendly as you," I promise. Bear is Dad's lead dog, a Newfoundland and Irish setter cross.

He barks once — deep as a lion baying — and looks out the cracked windshield.

I laugh and slam the door.

"See you, Bear."

Bear whines and sticks his massive head out the window. I blow him a final kiss and race after Dad and Tom. Tom is a cranky, gray-bearded dog racer with sled dogs to sell.

"Wait up, Dad," I shout.

This is the best day of my life. I've run Dad's team with him since before I can remember. And today I'm getting a team of my own.

We walk past Tom's log cabin and several sheds into

a clearing lined with rows of plywood doghouses. In front of each house is a long-legged husky chained to an iron stake. The dogs are hurling themselves around their stakes in circles, like kids on a merry-go-round. The smell of urine hangs in the air.

Tom doesn't say a word to his dogs, just plods past their houses.

"These dogs are valuable," he yells over the din. "They come from good racing lines."

The dog lot is filled with barks and yaps and snatches of howls. I put my mittens over my ears. The dogs all look the same — wild, gray blurs of movement. They seem like they've been bred to run, but not like they're used to being anyone's friend.

"Have you got any others?" I ask.

"I've got a few culls — dogs that I'm going to get rid of. Nothing worth selling, though."

We stop at the very end of the lot. Two silent dogs squat on top of their houses, as far back from us as they can reach. A scruffy black dog with white socks, however, dances on his back legs trying to reach me. He stares into my eyes and squeals like a puppy.

Tom chucks a cigarette butt on the snow and grinds it out with his heel.

"What do you think, Dad?" I ask.

But Dad's not listening. He's staring off toward the distant mountains, hands jammed in his overall pockets.

"I got these three from a friend who was leaving the Yukon," Tom continues. "They're not worth their feed, Becky. He couldn't get them to work."

I reach my hand out to the dancing dog.

"Hi," I whisper, scratching behind his ear. He crashes to a sit, sniffs my hand and leans against my legs. It's exactly what Bear does when I pat him.

"I want them," I say, walking over to the dogs on their houses. They both cringe.

"If you want to run dogs, get yourself a few pups. I have a litter almost ready to leave. These three are useless. They'll never pull for you. Hate to say it, but I'll probably end up shooting them."

Too late. I'm already unclipping their chains.

These dogs will pull for me, if I treat them right. This is the start of my team. I'm going to race them some day. And Dad's going to help me train them.

I'm going to build a team from these three culls. I'm going to learn how to train dogs by working with them. Then I'm going to breed them and keep running the best of their pups and grand-pups until I have at least fifteen of the fastest, friendliest racing dogs. By that time I'll be old enough to enter long races like the Quest.

The Quest runs every February over four mountain passes and along the Yukon River between Fairbanks, Alaska, and Whitehorse, Yukon. Winners usually finish the race in about eleven days. The racers camp out or sleep in bush cabins along the trail. Sometimes they travel together until the last stretch, cooking by bonfires under the northern lights.

And Dad? Well, he's going to be my handler. He promised me years ago when I first told him I wanted to race. Handlers and mushers are always close, he said. They have to be to take care of their dogs.

"Dad?" I say, my arms full of dog chains.

No answer.

The black-and-white dog leaps up, his paws on my chest.

But Dad's not looking at the mountains anymore.

He's staring at the ground.

1

"GET A stick, Becky," Dad yells over the din of his screaming dogs. They leap up on their back legs over and over, ready to run. "We can't keep waiting for you to catch up."

"No," I say. "They don't need sticks." It's our first day on the trail, and my shoulders and legs ache.

"Good luck then," says Dad.

Mum is out of sight breaking trail far ahead. Dad jumps on his toboggan runners and yanks his brake from the snow.

"Tighten up," he says to his line of six huskies. They lunge forward together, and the gang-lines snap tight. "Let's go! Hike up!"

Bear, Dad's lead dog, trots off, tail up. My lead dog, Ginger, circles in her harness. I sigh and jump off my runners, pushing the back of the sled.

"Tighten up," I say firmly.

Ginger lies down. Her white coat is hard to see against the snow. She has the long legs and high waist of a racing dog. She's built to run, but she's hard to train because she's so shy. If I make any sudden movements, she jerks away. I think she's been treated badly, or just not handled all that much. I don't want to yell at her or kick her like I've seen some mushers do. When she works, I'm going to give her a treat or pet her.

But first she has to stand up.

"Let's go," I call.

My middle dog, Pepper, leaps into the air. He was so hyper this morning that I had to get Dad to hold his head so I could wriggle the harness on. I've tied a scrap of leather to his collar so he can chew on it when he gets too excited. Otherwise he chews on his harness — that's partly why he got culled.

Pepper is black with a white mask and socks like a panda bear. Just looking at him makes me smile. When I first untied him, he didn't cringe. Instead, he knocked me down! He loves to run more than anything. He just doesn't love it yet when there's a toboggan dragging behind.

My wheel dog whimpers. Salt is skinny, not quite a year old but already skittish. He has gray and white fur, a pencil nose and blue eyes so light they shine like ice.

"Useless," muttered Tom the musher when he handed me Salt's chain. "Waste of time bothering with this one."

This morning I had to drag him, whimpering every step, to get him into harness. When I got him in place he just curled into a ball and the other two had to drag him to his feet. He whined and half howled for the first few minutes and then started to plod along — pulling to the side, then digging in his paws. His whines faded into choking gasps as Pepper's weight lurched him forward.

The thing is that the biggest, most muscular dog should be in the wheel-dog position next to the toboggan because that dog has to keep it running straight. And Salt is big-boned. If I can get him to put some weight on and work, his chest should be broad and deep.

"Hike up!" I shout louder.

Ginger stands and stretches. I can't reward her if she won't even walk!

My stomach is churning. Stay calm, I tell myself. Dad always says to stay calm, or the dogs will get overexcited and confused. Only yell at them as a last resort, or they'll never want to please you.

I walk up beside Ginger. She steps off the trail to avoid me. I grab her harness and walk with her until the other dogs and the sled are moving.

"Let's go," I repeat.

I want a lead dog like Bear, I think, as I sink into the soft snow beside the trail. One who comes to me and doesn't pull away. I want a lead dog I can trust.

My dogs plod on. I grab the handlebars as they slip past and jump on the runners, kicking with one boot, then the other. But whenever I stop kicking, my dogs stop, too.

Far ahead, I hear Dad shout at his dogs to whoa. When he sees me, he takes off again. Only Bear glances behind to see if I'm coming.

And that's how it is all day, my first day ever with my own team. Mile after mile, Dad's team waits. I kick and push, and my dogs inch along, tails between their legs.

2

OUT THE tent flap that evening I see Dad sleeping in the dog sled, the mountains slick with melting snow behind him. I guess it's the only place he can be alone. It tires him to talk. The toboggan is six feet long but so narrow he has to lie flat on his back.

My arms hurt. I ran my dogs twelve miles today. At least, I pushed on the handlebars from behind, since they hardly pulled.

Shivering, I drop another log in the stove. The wall tent cools off fast when the fire in the woodstove dies down. It's just canvas walls with a roof hole and tin safety for the stovepipe to jut through. No floor.

Last year I had to ride in the sled bag on Dad's toboggan with my little sister, Rachel, and her ginger-striped cat. Taffy acts like Rachel's her kitten. She follows her everywhere, except when Rachel tucks her into the sled bag. Dog mushing makes her spitting mad, I guess. No cat wants to be freight for a team of huskies!

We're heading back to our old mountain home now.

We've been gone for a year from the cabin we built on what used to be our trap-line.

Dad quit trapping a couple of years ago. "It's a dead way of life," he told Mum. "The bottom has dropped out of the fur market and lots of countries are banning the sale of fur altogether. The prices just aren't worth it anymore."

Dad used to be always laughing, but he wasn't laughing then. "Trouble is," he said, "that I've lived in the woods all my life. I don't know how to do anything else."

Then, when we came to town for the summer a year ago, Dad started staying on the couch all day with his cap over his eyes. He quit talking to me unless I asked him something, and then he just said yes or no. Sometimes Bear curled up on the floor beside the couch, but Dad didn't even talk to him.

Mum said that Dad's brain got sick. She said brains are like any other part of the body. Your leg can get b roken and so can your brain. She said Dad isn't sad because of anything we did to him or because he doesn't love us anymore. He's just sad because his brain's sick.

There's a word for his sickness. It's called depression.

Until this year, we'd go back home to the bush every fall, and I'd go to school by correspondence. It only took the mornings, and in the afternoons I could go fishing or build forts in the woods with Rachel.

Lots of time we didn't even have school because we were too busy traveling with our dog team around the trap-line.

Mum doesn't like noisy dogs, so when we travel she always breaks trail up ahead, where it's quiet. She's a carver, and she likes to look around when she's snowshoeing and get ideas. Then she sketches them quickly at night in the tent and uses the drawings to make carvings when she has more time.

Mum's carvings are different from anything I've seen. She splits a slab of firewood — spruce or birch — and pencils in the pictures she's drawn on paper. Then she takes a pocketknife and carves around the drawing on the wood, until the picture on the slab stands out in relief. She never uses paint, but if she wants a bit of her carving darker, she burns it. Mum loves things simple, she says. Just black and white and the natural grain and smell of the wood.

This trip is important to Mum because the owner of the new gallery in town asked her to sell him a series of carvings based on family life and traveling in the bush. She's supposed to get them ready for tourist season when we go back to town next month.

The trip is special to me for other reasons. To begin with, I'm running my own team for the first time. Mostly, though, this trip feels special because Dad's depressed. Mum told us that he has to rest and he can't stand any stress or noise. She said being in the mountains helps people get over depression sometimes. It makes them feel at peace.

But Mum didn't tell us everything. I heard her one night when Dad wasn't home and she thought I was asleep. Her back was to me and she was talking to a friend on the phone.

"I don't know what I'll do if this trip doesn't help him," she said.

There was silence for a minute.

"He'd be better off by himself. And it would be easier on the girls."

She paused again. "This new medicine might do something. The others haven't done any good and nor have I."

I ran back to bed and put a pillow over my head so I wouldn't hear anymore. Some time in the night, Bear poked his wet nose into my face and I let him climb onto my bed. That night I slept scrunched against the wall, Bear snoring happily by my side.

We can take one week to mush to the cabin on this trip. Then we'll have about three weeks there at the very most before we'll have to head back to town. If we wait any longer, there's a good chance that the snow will have melted and the dogs won't be able to pull the toboggan. Mum says break-up is coming earlier every year.

A month for Dad to get better. That's all.

Mum told us that it's hard for Dad to get better because he feels his depression has let everybody down.

The medication should work, she told us, if only he has a bit of time to relax.

"It would be a big help, Becky," she said, "if you would leave those dogs of yours behind for this trip. They're noisy and they don't know how to work."

"I can't," I said. "They need the training."

"There's no room on the toboggan for their feed."

"Then I'll pack it on my toboggan."

"It will be hard on Dad."

"He won't even notice they're there."

Or maybe he will when he sees me training my own team, I think, but I'm not telling that to anyone yet.

Besides, I can't leave the dogs behind because of a secret I can't even tell Mum. Ginger is going to have pups soon. She's huge, and if Mum and Dad ever looked at her properly they'd notice right off.

I don't know who the father of the pups is. I don't even know if she was already pregnant when I got her. Really, I shouldn't be bringing her with me. There won't be room on the sled to take a litter of pups back to town. But I don't know anyone who would take proper care of Ginger. If she doesn't bond with me when she has her pups, then she won't let me near them and they won't grow up trusting people, either.

And if I don't train her on this trip I won't have her ready to help train her puppies next winter. A well-trained lead dog shows new dogs what they should be doing.

•••

Tonight is our first night in the wall tent. I've already chopped spruce boughs for dog beds. I limbed my first tree and helped Mum pack the lengths back to the tent. Tomorrow she said I could chop the kindling.

Mum has propped up a length of spruce so one end is resting on a stump.

She's swede-sawing it into stove-length chunks, and Dad's sleeping in his toboggan.

My dogs are fed and staked by Dad's.

Rachel is walking on her hands from dog to dog, patting them with her feet. Bear is following her, whining, because he can't figure out what she's doing. She's fresh because she just sat in the sled bag on top of Dad's load all day. She's also mad because she doesn't want to be here.

She'd rather be in town going to gymnastics lessons. That's all she thinks about these days, so she's sure not going to make the trip any easier by helping out.

When I was little, Dad used to tell me that we would go on trips together and I could help run Bear and the rest of his team until I was ready to handle my own. He said that of course girls could run dogs and even win tough races like the Quest.

But Dad's dogs are work dogs, freighting dogs — the kind trappers have always used in the bush. They're way too big for racing. Dad said the days of the freighting dogs are as dead as the days of the old-timers, the bushmen, but that when I got older I could breed my own smaller long-legged huskies for racing if that was what I wanted. He said smaller dogs tend to recover faster when they're worn out. They find it easier to get their heart back.

Well, I'm breeding those dogs now! I don't know about the father, but Ginger is long-legged and thin and quick. I'm old enough to be responsible for pups if I can mush twelve miles in a day, like I did today.

And if I can get my team working smoothly and following my commands, Dad will be sure to notice.

3

IT'S COLD. I grope for my hat, shove it on and sit up. The floor is just snow covered with caribou hides and sleeping bags. I'm on the outside nearest the tent flap. Next to me are the stove, an armful of split wood and a box of gear. Dishes are piled on a couple of stumps that double as chairs. Dad made the wood stove rectangular so it's easy to cook on. It's small enough to pack on the toboggan with the pipes nestled in the firebox.

I can tell the fire's out because the tin isn't glowing anymore. A half-drunk cup of tea is frozen on the ground.

The rest of the family's sleeping, but I'm not going to lie in bed waiting for Mum and Dad to wake up this year. I jump up and open the tent flap. Salt and Ginger are curled up beside each other, and Pepper's legs are twitching in his sleep. The northern lights are green and cranberry red, dancing across the sky and over the mountains down valley where we're heading to the cabin.

I head over to Bear and whistle. He uncurls from the hole he's dug in the snow and jumps up so his feet rest on my shoulders. I kiss his nose, the way I've done every morning of my life for as long as I can remember.

"Back to sleep, Bear," I say. He lies down again and tucks his huge head under his tail.

I stand still and listen. Dad says when the sky's very clear you can hear the lights crackle. The moon is over the creek and I hear the water running way below the ice. It's funny how water sounds in the winter. When I hear it move through the darkness it sounds so near, but Mum can chop down several feet before she hits water. When it's that far under the ice, the pressure makes the water shoot up and flood the hole. Sometimes, though, it's too far down, and we have to melt snow. Snow water never tastes as good. Besides, it takes buckets and buckets to melt enough for the five-gallon dog food pot.

I decide to make the fire myself today. I grab the brush from the heap piled by the door and bring it inside. Then I light a candle and kneel in front of the stove. Outside, Pepper barks happily in his sleep, as if he's chasing something.

I've never lit the morning fire in the tent before, because Mum and Dad always woke up first. I open the drafts and the tin door like I've seen them do hundreds of times. Then I scrunch the brush up into splinters in my hand and heap it on the ashes. I hold the candle under the heap until it catches the flame.

"Thanks," says Dad from his caribou hide.

I look over at him. He's lying in the candlelight with his arms under his neck, watching me.

"I was cold," he says.

His voice is peaceful. He hardly ever says anything to me anymore unless he thinks I'm training my dogs wrong. Maybe Mum was right and this trip will help him. After a day on the trail he already looks more like his old self. Or maybe he's just noticing that I'm helping out. He always wanted me to be capable in the bush so I could do things with him.

I'm too short to hang onto the handlebars properly. I stand on the runners, clutching the handlebars tight with Dad balanced behind me. The spring sunshine is hot on my face and the dogs' collars click along to the swish of the runners on the wet snow. Snow slides from a spruce tree with a loud thump. Dad and I are singing.

Then, without warning, he jumps off and is standing behind me on the trail, laughing.

"Whoa!" I call out calmly, so Bear won't get spooked.

"Bye, Becky," says Dad. "I'm walking home. I'll see you there."

I open my mouth to tell him no, but "hike up," comes out instead. Bear leans into his traces, and the team pulls out the toboggan. I stand on the runners scared to let go, but I'm singing as I head back to the cabin, just me and the dogs and the sunshine on the snow…

Outside the tent, I fill the coffee pot with snow. Candlelight shines through the tent walls. The aurora is sparking the whole sky now with spears like flash fires in a dry wood. The dogs are restless. Ginger paws at her snow burrow and whimpers before curling back into a ball with her tail covering her nose. I kneel down and rumple her neck ruff.

"Hey, pups," I whisper into her ear. It twitches, but Ginger doesn't move.

I put the coffeepot on the back of the stove and boil coffee for Dad, then pour it in his mug with Trumilk and sugar and hand it to him. He sits up and takes the cup. I fix myself tea and we sit side by side until the sun rises over the mountains and the white-feathered ptarmigan are cackling in the willows and sunlight floods through the white walls of the tent.

•••

Mum has already stamped out a snowshoe trail for the first mile or so this morning. The dogs are too wild when they're first hooked up to stay behind Mum without stepping on the backs of her snowshoes.

In the afternoon, though, it gets hot — too hot for the dogs. Northern dogs have such thick fur coats that they can't bear to work when the temperature rises anywhere close to melting. They dehydrate way too fast.

Now we're running them along the river ice with Mum ahead breaking trail. She's walking wide-legged in her snowshoes and feels in front of her by poking at the ice with a spruce pole. Dad is behind her with the big team and Rachel and the cat are in the sled bag where all the gear is lashed down. Ahead I can hear Rachel explaining to the cat how to spring into a handstand from a backwards somersault.

I'm last in line mushing Ginger, Pepper and Salt. Pepper has got his traces tight, at least, but the other two aren't pulling. Ginger is following the trail but her heart isn't in it. She's holding her head high — a sure sign that she's not working hard. Salt is trying to run backwards and Pepper is barking frantically at a moose track that is luckily going in our direction. If the moose parts company with the trail, Pepper's likely to follow. Desperate with excitement, he snaps over and over at the piece of leather I've hung to his harness.

"No, Salt," I call out, for the fiftieth time. He just continues to twist around in his harness, and the toboggan careens from side to side as he turns. Salt skids along facing me and screaming until the other dogs stop, confused. I begin to hope that Pepper bites him. The harnesses tangle and I have to stop and sort out the lines while hanging on to Pepper with one hand so he doesn't make it worse.

Mum and Dad are, of course, way ahead. I see them talking on the ice but can't make out anything over Salt's screams. I'm not sure if he's scared or he just doesn't want to pull. I'm also not sure if I can teach him anything. When I used to help Dad with new dogs, they learned lots from the rest of the team, but I don't have a single dog who knows what he's doing.

Then Mum moves on and we round a corner and there's overflow from bank to bank — water running over the more solid ice below. Mum unbuckles her snowshoes and wades out into it. I can see it go over her boots and I'm nervous because I'll have to go through it, too. I don't even know if my dogs will pull through the water. Some dogs are afraid of overflow and have to be led across. Ginger looks like she's ready to bolt back to me.

"Whoa," shouts Dad. He's already got his team out in the water so I don't know why he's stopping them now. They won't want to get going again. But Mum is wading back and they're standing beside Bear. He's lying on his side in the water and they're leaning over him.

I take a deep breath and hold it. Not Bear.

Bear is beautiful and huge — close to 120 pounds and black with red plumes on his tail. He's got a massive chest and long runner's legs. Dad thinks he's perfect — the strength of a Newfoundland dog with the energy and brains of a setter, he told me once. We've had him since he was a puppy, barely old enough to waddle. He was the runt of his litter. Dad says I picked him out, but I can't remember. I wasn't much more than a baby like him.

Dad unclips Bear's traces and carries him, staggering, to the main toboggan. He lays him carefully on top of the load in front of Rachel, and Bear just lies there on his side, panting.

All of a sudden, his panting is very loud. It seems to fill the whole valley. It's very hot and the snow is falling off the spruce trees in great whumps along the bank. Foam is coming out of Bear's mouth and his breath doesn't sound like breath. It sounds like gurgling and wheezing together, and I know he's going to die.

I know, too, that Dad's not supposed to have any stress on this trip and that Bear's been his lead dog since he started to run a team.

"Let's go," Dad hollers at his dogs. Egypt is the lead dog now. She turns her head and stares at him. She's black and long-legged and slim. Dad got her last year to breed with Bear when she's a bit older, but she's never had to work in lead position before, and she has no idea what to do. Mum starts to haul her forward by the collar. Egypt whines and when she stops, the panting from Bear sounds even louder.

Ginger, Pepper and Salt slide a little farther forward on the ice, so I'm standing in the water. Salt digs in his claws and whines, leaning backwards. Overflow trickles into my boots and splashes up my pants. One mitten is wet, too, but nobody's paying any attention to me.

If this had happened any other year, Mum and Dad would have been talking to Rachel and me the whole time, telling us not to worry, that they had everything under control.

Mum walks ahead of the team again, but this time instead of tapping on the ice, she walks backwards, calling to Egypt.

"Come on, girl. Let's go."

The dogs don't want to go. When Bear's in lead, Dad has to holler to hold them back. His dogs almost drag him off his feet when he puts them in harness. He has to tie them to trees so they won't break out the load before he's ready, but now without Bear they just stand with the traces slack and their tails between their legs.

"Let's go," Dad shouts again. This year, he's hardly yelled anything at them. Other years, he used to shout most of the day. Sometimes he was mad and sometimes he was just encouraging them, but he was always talking or whistling to them. This year he mostly stands on the back of his sled and waits until they take him somewhere.

Dad told me once that without their lead dog, a team has no heart.

Suddenly, I'm glad I've brought Ginger along, even pregnant. My team's going to have heart.

The toboggans go a way down the river like this, Mum walking backwards, Bear screaming and frothing on top of the load, and me walking beside my little sled hanging onto Salt's collar so he's forced to face frontward.

"I want to get down," Rachel shouts, sounding panicked. "I don't want to be with Bear."

"Stay where you are," Mum says. "There's nowhere else for you to go."

"No," yells Rachel, crying. "Let me out."

Mum says something back to her but I can't make out the words because Bear's screams sound like they're quicker and closer together. And all of a sudden I'm cold, even though my face is burning. I've never seen a dog of ours carried on a sled before.

"Whoa," Dad yells.

Suddenly I forget about my dogs and that they might get tangled in their harness or fight if I leave them. I forget that a caribou or moose could wander by and my dogs could take off after it and I might not get them back. Instead I run to Mum and she puts her arms around me and we stand there in the boot-deep overflow and try not to listen to Bear's screams.

"Mummy," says Rachel, "please help me out." She's standing on top of her sleeping bag nest with her face smudged from tears.

Mum and I walk over to her and Mum lifts her out. Dad is taking his rifle out of the scabbard and the sun shines hot over the river ice.

"Bear's heart must be giving out," Mum tells us. "Sometimes it happens to sled dogs suddenly like this. No one knows exactly why. Sled-dog myopathy, it's called."

Dad picks up Bear in his arms. Dad's shoulders sag. Bear spills over his arms, his head hanging down.

I let go of Mum. I pick up that huge head and scratch behind his ears and kiss his nose.

"Bye, Bear," I whisper.

Bear whimpers. As gently as I can I let his head go, and Dad walks back along our trail. He hasn't cradled Bear since he was a pup.

I look back and watch them getting smaller and smaller. Rachel stands on top of the sled, her curls sticking up in damp spikes around her head. Mum puts her arms around us both and I don't even think that I'm too old.

I hide my face until I hear the gunshot.

Then another.

"Take it easy," says Mum. "Take it easy, girls. This way Bear won't be suffering."

Dad walks over to a tree and buries his face. Then he does a strange thing. He pounds the tree with both fists.

I can't watch. I rub my mittens against my eyes.

When I can finally look again, Dad is walking back to us.

"Did you have to shoot him?" Rachel demands, her face twisted and furious. "He could have got better."

"He wouldn't," says Dad. His face looks like it did in town before we left on this trip. It's hard and closed like a slammed door. His trail leads to a sweeper, a spruce tree hanging over the bank, and under it is a black mound.

Dad puts a chain on Egypt.

We can't be leaving. Bear can't be staying here alone.

When I was a baby I used to ride on his back. When Dad was first training him, he put me in the sled for weight. Why are we just going on like nothing's changed?

"Sorry, girls," says Mum. "We can't stand around here in the water anymore. We might as well get moving." She takes the end of the chain from Dad and snowshoes ahead. Rachel puts her thumb in her mouth and climbs back on the sled to hold the cat. Let Taffy cuddle with her just this once, I mutter to myself, and I push on my sled.

Salt is facing forward, although every couple of minutes he glances back at the toboggan longingly.

"No!" I shout, and he swivels forward again. Ginger has her head down now and Pepper is grunting as he pulls, still to one side. I keep pushing but whenever I hop on the runners my dogs stop. Ginger stands looking straight ahead, and Pepper rears on his back legs and lunges forward over and over to pull out the toboggan. Salt sits down.

"Let's go!" I shout each time. They might not be working much but at least they're following Dad's team.

What's left of it, that is.

•••

We're camped beside the river tonight, where a mountain rises straight from its bank. We're across from a bluff and Mum says there won't be any sun in the morning.

Dad set up the tent while Rachel unloaded our gear from the toboggan. I helped Mum saw up two dead spruce for firewood and made spruce bough beds for all the dogs. It saves on dog food if they're sleeping off the snow. Besides, it's way more comfortable. Dog food is usually the heaviest part of the gear on a long trip.

"Think there's enough boughs for Egypt?" I asked Dad, when I was piling hers. But he was threading the stovepipe through the tent safety and didn't answer.

I chopped until the moon rose and the stars came out. Whenever I stopped working, I remembered Bear lying still warm in the snow.

Dad is sitting outside on a stump, smoking. He promised to quit before he got depressed, but now he's smoking more than ever. He taps it out, stores the butt in his shirt pocket in case his tobacco runs out and puts his head in his hands.

Mum is drinking tea in the candlelight and trying to haywire a toboggan brake back together. Her sketching pencil is stuck behind her ear where she always keeps it, but I know she won't sketch any scenes from today.

Rachel is drawing a picture in her journal, though. She draws a mountain and spruce trees and a river and a yellow sun. I don't wait around to see if she'll put Bear in the picture.

I go outside and lean on Dad's shoulder. He doesn't react. He smells like tobacco and sweat. That's the strange thing. He still smells like Dad.

"Dad," I ask him, "wasn't there anything we could do? Shouldn't we have tried to save him?"

He doesn't even look up at me. The moon is over the peaks now and I can hear the water running under the ice, but Dad isn't listening.

What will happen if he doesn't get better on this trip? Will Mum really ask him to leave us? Would it be better for Rachel and me? Would it make any difference if I really tried hard to please him on the trail?

After a long time he says something, and his voice is so soft I strain to listen. "It doesn't matter," I think he says. "He just died."

I wouldn't let Ginger go without a fight. I'd have put up the tent and brought her in where it was warm. When a dog dies during the Quest, the musher places him in the sled and carries him to the next checkpoint. Lots of mushers scratch when a dog dies. Even if there's nothing they could have done, they don't have the heart to continue.

I keep leaning against Dad's shoulder, but it doesn't matter.

He's really not there.

4

THE NEXT morning, I wake up in the dark and lie still, remembering Bear.

I'm playing with stuffed animals when Dad brings in Bear.

"Becky," he says, "you'll need your boots on. Your stuffies can watch." He lines my stuffies on my bunk and whistles Bear over. "Get on him like you're going for a ride on his back."

I stand over Bear, barely able to reach the floor with my boots on.

Dad hands me the harness. "Slip the orange collar over his head and the traces under his front legs. See? Watch."

Dad shows me and I position the harness the way he shows.

"No, no," he laughs. "You've got his head in the leg hole. See the X the traces make? That has to be over his back."

For days, I harness stuffed animals, dolls and mostly Rachel, who wriggles and shakes her head on command. Whenever Dad takes out his team that winter, he gets me to harness Bear. During cold snaps, Rachel and I bring in Bear. We line him up with our stuffed animals as his teammates, and they run races around the kitchen table.

In the tent I lie shivering and think about calling Mum and Dad to light the stove. Instead I grope for a candle, pull on my clothes in the sleeping bag and push open the tent flap. I wipe a few hairs from my caribou hide off my face. The hairs are hollow and incredibly warm to sleep on, but they fall out easily, and after a few days on the trail there's even hair in our tea and supper.

I go out and stand by Ginger's spruce bough bed.

"Hey, pups! Hey, Ginger!" I whisper. I can't ever remember not calling Bear when I wake up.

The sky is salted with stars. Today will be a better day, I think. Nothing more can go wrong.

Ginger stands, stretches and pokes her muzzle into my hand. She's never come to me on her own before! These dogs are all I've got now.

Ginger's white fur shines in the moonlight. Last night when we made camp, she pawed the harness over her head and stepped out of the traces. Then she bolted for the tent and tried to hide. I was proud of her. None of Dad's dogs ever slipped off their harness. Ginger's long nose makes her look like she has some collie in her.

I bet she's really smart. Dad said once that some of the best lead dogs ever had collie in them.

It's only a matter of time before Mum and Dad see she's pregnant.

I scratch at her nose, and her slanted eyes glow in the dark.

Then, above the bluff across the river ice, I hear a wolf call. I listen, the willows crouched like a wall around me. The dogs perk up their ears but don't move. They don't want to draw attention to themselves.

After a few minutes, I gather up the dogs' pots and the pail we boiled dog food in over the campfire last night. I pick up the ax and swede saw and rope up my own toboggan by the light of a candle stuck in a tobacco can lid on a stump. If Dad's going to help me train my new pups for racing, he'll need to know that I'm capable of doing chores alone.

The wolf is calling again and again from the cliff top.

Our dogs will bark if a moose or caribou wanders by, but sometimes they just go quiet for wolves. I've seen Mum and Dad handle wolf packs around the dogs before. They shout every so often and keep on with whatever they're doing.

"Get," I yell toward the cliff.

Under the tobacco can is my map. I studied it last night trying to pick out today's route. When I find a mountain with three peaks in a straight line, that means we turn north.

A wind rattles the willows and lifts snow off the river ice. The northern lights are a smudge against the cliff. Then the lights burst white and green across the sky, flashing and dying out like firebrands thrust into dark water.

I kick at the ashes of last night's dog food fire. Embers glow in the depression surrounded by snow, and smoke whips over the clearing and along the river. The air smells warm, like willows in the spring. I break lichen-covered brush off the spruce tree and heap it loosely on the embers.

Then I see it — a black wolf with slanted-back eyes like Ginger's, long-legged and gangly — across the river, down from the cliff. It's watching our camp and, at once, the dogs are standing, turned toward the dark willows. The lights are changing color now, shades of crocus blue and fireweed pink, flashing into flame and dying out above the mountains.

Now the wolves are crossing the river ice side by side, climbing the bank. The dogs crouch against the trees and the wolves stand ranged before me, so close I can see the shining of their eyes. Bear would have growled and barked. He always warned us when wolves were near.

I toss another armful of brush on the flames.

"Get out of here," I growl like Dad would, and the fire throws shadows over the snow. And suddenly, the wolves are gone, shapes moving through the bush and then, moments later, stepping single file across the ice.

The dogs haven't made a sound, but Salt whimpers now from his snow burrow. When the wolves can no longer be seen, he stands and barks fiercely in the direction they've vanished, then curls up again with his tail over his head. Impressed, Pepper lurches to his feet and barks at the invisible wolves.

"Good dog," I say, patting his back. Pepper hurls his front feet on my shoulders and knocks me over, laughing, in the snow.

•••

It's light but Mum was right. The cliffs are blocking the sunlight this morning. Dad's outside on a stump, of course, and the rest of us are eating bannock — fried baking powder bread. This morning it's crisp on the outside and smeared with cranberry jam.

I can't get that phone call to Mum's friend out of my mind. She said she couldn't live with Dad depressed anymore. I wonder if he knows this trip is his last chance. With Bear dead now, how can he possible feel better?

"We can be at the cabin in four days if we hurry," says Mum. "We've got enough food to stay there for a few weeks."

"If it stays hot during the day like this," I say, "the

snow might not last that long. We can't run the dogs without snow." Pepper is shaking the tree he's tied to. When snow falls from its branches, he attacks the snow.

"If the snow melts while we're at the cabin," says Mum, "we'll use dog packs for our gear. The dogs can pack on the trip out. It'll be a circus walking with all the dogs loose, but we won't have so much dog or people food to carry."

Dog packs are two bags connected by straps under the dog's chest and over its back. As long as the two sides are weighted evenly, the dogs don't seem to notice. Trouble is, of course, that sled dogs overheat in the warm weather and love nothing better than splashing into a creek. Gear and food that need to stay dry are best left in people packs.

"How many dog packs have we got?" asks Rachel, trying to sound grown-up.

"Three. But there's enough leather at the cabin to sew packs for the rest of the dogs. Do you feel like helping to sew them?"

"I can pack gear, too," says Rachel, straightening her forty pounds of sheer muscle.

"I cut up the leather for wall tent patches a year ago," Dad says from his stump outside. "Besides, I don't want to leave the sled behind."

I'd forgotten he was there. Wait until he realizes he's got a litter of pups to get back to town, too.

And for the first time I wonder, what if Mum and Dad just won't bring those pups?

•••

We're heading over a new pass. I'm right behind Mum with Ginger, Pepper and Salt. Ginger's trail is much softer now because she's only following a single set of snowshoe tracks, not the road that Dad's team and toboggan gouge out. And yet she's pulling now with her head bowed and her back humped.

"Such a good dog," I call. "Aren't you lovely?" It sounds silly to keep talking to her but I want my lead dog to pay attention to my voice. I'm proud of her and scared for her pups at the same time. This is the first time I've gone ahead of Dad's big toboggan. He's following behind because he hasn't got a lead dog anymore, and the only way to hurry Egypt is to have me ahead. Dad doesn't like it much but he doesn't say anything.

"What if your dogs start chasing a caribou?" he said before we left the tent site. "You're not strong enough to hold them. And your dogs don't know how to listen. They need discipline."

"They won't bolt," I said. "I'm training them."

"Whatever," he muttered.

Then he strung a rope between Egypt's collar and my handlebars so she'd be forced to keep up.

More than anything I want to untie that rope. When

I'm racing I'll be on my own. Dad will only be waiting to help when my team pulls into the checkpoints.

"I'll watch out for caribou," Rachel called cheerfully from her upside-down position in the snow. "I'll help Becky if her dogs run off." She leapt out of her handstand and threw her arms in the air in a victory salute. "Mum," she shouted. "The crust's thick enough for me to do handstands!"

Rachel has the attention span of a snow flea, but I sure wish I could do handstands like that. I decide to practice when no one is looking.

On the trail I make sure that the rope between the sleds is slack, shout to Dad what I'm doing, then jump on my brake with both feet. The brake is a square chunk of iron hinged to the back of the sled where I stand so I can kick it off like an anchor. I need to be sure that Ginger will stop when I tell her and so far she never has. When I get the toboggan stopped, I get off and pet her while Dad puts his head down and doesn't speak. The rope trailing between my sled and Dad's team is awkward. I have to keep jumping out of its way.

Rachel yells encouraging comments from her sleeping bag nest.

"They're getting better," she yells. "Salt is going forwards!"

We drink a thermos of tea and then get going again. The mountains are closing up on either side of the river. Mum and I are searching for a creek coming in from the north. It isn't as simple as it sounds because sloughs often come into the main channel of a river at right angles, too.

"This is it," I yell. "Whoa," I call to Ginger and flop the brake down off the back of the sled. I jump on it with all my might and bear down.

"Good work," yells Rachel. I look back. She's kneeling on top of the load, her cheeks rosy from the sun.

Mum stops and unfolds the map from her pocket. She snowshoes back on the trail. "I think Becky's right," she tells Dad.

Of course I'm right, I think.

Dad looks sick. His face has no color and it's tight like when he's trying not to get angry.

"Your team needs to keep going," he snaps. "You can't keep stopping them. We'll never get anywhere."

I look away from him. When Dad first let me give commands to his team, I shouted whoa to Bear every five minutes, and he just laughed.

"You said they don't know how to listen," I tell him quietly. "I'm teaching them how."

Dad shrugs. "Suit yourself," he mutters.

"What's wrong with him?" mutters Dad, walking along the line of dogs. I stand on the runners in the wind, kicking my boots to keep warm. "Tighten up," orders Dad, turning Bear by the harness so he's facing the trail.

Dad jumps back on the toboggan.

Bear veers to the left. We're on the river and the ice looks just fine, but Dad lets Bear go his own route.

On the way home we run the dogs by the same spot. The ice where Bear refused to go has fallen in. The open water is deep and very fast.

"If I'd lost my temper," says Dad quietly, "he might have done what I asked. We'd probably be dead. The musher is the boss, Becky, but only if you treat your dogs with respect."

Mum looks at Dad for a long time and I notice he doesn't look back at her.

"Are you okay?" she asks.

He just stares off at the mountains. All the fun of the sunshine and my finding the way and Salt pulling forwards seem to blow away.

"The doctor said it takes at least four weeks for the new medicine to work," Mum says to him softly.

"Whatever," says Dad again.

I wonder if he hurts her feelings. He used to be her best friend, she told me once. She told me if I ever got married, I should marry my best friend.

Dad takes his tobacco out of his pocket and rolls a smoke.

It's not like flu, Mum said, when she first told me about depression. You can't catch it from someone.

So why do I feel it — like a heaviness hanging in the air?

5

WE MUSH up the creek to the north, slowing gradually to a walk as the dogs tire. Ginger is pulling just enough to keep the traces tight, but that's too much on the freshly broken trail. With pups inside her, she probably shouldn't be working at all. If something happens to her it will be my fault.

Salt has had enough for the day. He walks along with his tail tucked between his legs and stops every few minutes to turn and whine at me until he gets jerked ahead by the others.

Pepper is working with all his might, but he's still frustrated, pulling to one side so the toboggan can't follow properly. It keeps getting pulled off the ruts of Mum's snowshoe trail. It's called dog-tracking, Dad told me once, and it's really hard to cure. A dog does it when the rest of the team is going too slow for his liking. I'm not sure what I can do about it except get the others working faster.

"Let's go, dogs," I call out again and again.

We're starting on a shortcut over to the next river valley that should save sixteen miles. Dad and Mum used to joke that their shortcuts always took longer than their regular routes. Dad said once that you should never run dogs through a new pass without checking it out first on foot. We've run into too many side-hills that way and had to run the toboggan at an angle across slopes so steep that Mum's been scared to look back. Sometimes only Bear's massive build kept the toboggan from hurtling down.

But I'm not going to worry about that now. I want to think about something besides Bear. Maybe a new pass will distract everyone.

Besides, I've always loved not knowing where I'm going exactly. It makes me feel free. That's why I want to be a dog musher. More than winning a race, it's the feel of sunshine on spring snow and the mountains opening up in all directions.

And maybe one more thing. I love to watch dogs run. I can almost feel myself running with them, light and happy and free.

The sun is traveling across the sky, and the creek we're following curves through sheer cliffs on both sides, farther and farther up toward a pass.

I see it first — a bald eagle soaring above the last of the spruce trees just before we climb out of the timber.

"Look," Rachel yells from the sled bag. "I see its nest."

"Whoa," I shout and forget about the brake.

Ginger stops! I knew she was smart. Then she rolls on her back to scratch and tangles the harness.

"Good girl," I tell her for stopping. Then, "No," I say, for rolling over.

Ginger stops, looking puzzled. I stand her back on her feet. I'll have to remember about giving one order at a time!

"It's an eyrie," I call back to Rachel. "See? In the tree." The nest is so huge that it looks like the spruce tree might collapse. In the next tree is another bald eagle, its white head glistening in the sunlight. Even Dad is looking and, as we watch, the eagle moves its wings and is in the air.

I can see its wings spread out almost as wide as Rachel is tall. The eagle flies right at its mate and they soar high over the cliffs above the creek and tumble back toward us, riding an air wave. It looks like their talons are stuck together, but it happens too fast to be sure. Near the ground, they separate and soar up again, their nest a shaky mess of sticks and moss, almost as big as one of our line cabins. It looks like a beaver feed pile stuck up in a tree.

The spring sunshine's hot and the snow is blowing off the spruce boughs and blasting around. We all start to laugh. Even Dad is perched beside Rachel on the dog sled, holding the binoculars for her and pointing. His face isn't tight anymore and as the eagles ride a down-draft over our heads, he laughs again.

I haven't heard him laugh all year.

I snap my sled to a tree with the dog chain. Pepper is whining to get going and making desperate leaps in the air. Salt is curled up in a gray heap hoping I won't notice him. Ginger lies down on her side with a grunt, sunbathing on the melting snow.

I walk along my line of dogs and hug each one

"Here," says Dad, handing me the binoculars. I focus on the nest. Feathers are stuck among the sticks. "Bald eagles come back to their nests year after year," he says. "They just keep renovating until it or the tree falls down."

I know all this but I like to hear him talking.

Dad pulls the thermos and the jerky out of the sled bag and we sit on the toboggan in the sunshine and blowing wind and have a break.

A month. Mum said the medicine could take at least a month and we might not even have that long for this trip. Maybe she's right, though, I think, looking at his face. Maybe being in the mountains does make people feel better.

Then I remember that we'll have climbed above timberline when it's time to make camp tonight. There won't be any spruce trees that high. So I untie the ax from my sled and chop spruce boughs — only a few from each tree so it won't die. I make a pile for dogs' beds and then a pile for us to place under our caribou hides. I've never been allowed to use the ax other years, but this time I've brought along my own. I decided that

I couldn't have my own team without my own hatchet! I'll need it for everything, from making dog beds to cutting trail.

Nobody stops me, though Mum watches pretty closely.

I strap the heap of boughs on my sled on top of my load while Mum and Dad sip tea. From the corner of my eye I watch Taffy stalk headfirst from the sled bag, pause frozen a moment and then leap onto the snow. She streaks away from the toboggan with Rachel running after her.

"Run," Dad tells Taffy, as Rachel leaps on the cat.

"Got her!" shouts Rachel. She shoves the spitting cat back in the sled bag out of the eyes of the soaring eagles. Mum puts away the thermos and buckles on her snowshoes.

Dad wanted to name the cat Madness when we first got her because he said it was madness to take a cat on dog-mushing trips. He said there wasn't an expedition in history that carried cats in the load. Mum said there wasn't one that carried kids, either, and Rachel said the explorers must have had boring adventures then. When we were little we even carried our plastic dolls in the sled, but they would smash in cold temperatures whenever we hit a tree.

"Let's go," I shout at Ginger. She creaks to her feet and waddles along with her traces hanging slack, barely moving in the heat.

My throat feels tight. I hope she makes it to the cabin before the pups are born. If she has her pups on the trail, would Dad even agree to wait?

A load of snow thumps off a scrubby spruce tree. Pepper leaps in the air and bites at it as the snow wallops his furry head. He leaps to one side and my toboggan begins to flip. I push it up again, breathing hard. The snow must be heavy because it's full of water, beginning to melt. Spring is coming more quickly than we'd planned.

Dad's dogs are trotting behind my sled, whining because they want us to go faster. The toboggans are gouging a trail right down to the base of the soft, wet snow.

•••

We're camping high in the mountains tonight. The chinook has blown over and a half-moon is throwing shadows over the snow. There are no spruce trees here, only willow and scrub birch — buck brush — growing in clumps with open areas between them.

We had to search a long while before we made camp, hoping to find dry, flat ground. Mum says there's ice beneath the snow in our tent. If we camp here more than one night, the tent ground will be one huge mud puddle. Rachel ought to love that! A puddle is already forming beside the stove, the tin legs sinking, slanting the stove into the meltwater.

Dad's sitting on a stack of willow firewood in front of the tent flap, looking over the peaks, the ptarmigan cackling like mad chickens on the overflow ice, chasing each other, their feet scratching the snow.

Rachel is drawing in her journal — a stick tree with a round black nest.

"Maybe there's eggs in the nest?" Rachel asks me. She sits with her legs stretched open in front of her, the notebook resting on her knees. Her cheeks are sunburned and chubby, her long curls tucked behind her ears.

Rachel's cute. People just smile when she talks to them.

"I don't know," I tell her. "I couldn't see into it." I'm drawing, too, but my page is getting cluttered. There's a tent and a candle burning on a stump and river ice and a black wolf watching the campfire. The sky I fill with colored lights bursting across the dark. I don't know how to show the wind.

I start again — another page — and there's Dad perched on the dog sled laughing, and sunshine is spilling through the forest.

"I like it," says Mum, flipping a bannock. She hasn't even unpacked her sketching pad. That's not like Mum. Usually she hates to cook when she's got a project in mind. If she does, the food burns.

The bannock is a perfect golden color.

"Becky." Dad calls from his willow stack.

"Yes."

"If wolves come to the tent again, do you think you could wake me up?"

I can see him through the tent flap in the moonlight. He's looking right at me for a change when he talks. I can't see him clearly but it looks like maybe he's smiling.

Tomorrow I'm going to look for lowbush cranberries. They grow right down in the moss. They ripen in the fall but the leaves and berries stay on the plant until spring, no matter how cold the winter. I'll have to find the right slope and clear away the snow, and underneath I should find them as fresh as before winter came.

The willows are yellow and the sky is blue. Sunshine warms my face and head, but my fingers are stiff from picking berries on the frosty ground. In the distance, smoke puffs from the cabin stovepipe and drifts across the clearing into the forest. I'm not allowed to go any farther than this alone.

Suddenly, I'm nervous.

"Bear," I call, and he lifts his head from the moss where he, too, is picking cranberries. He ambles over to me and we lie on the ground, my face to the sun, Bear's huge head resting on my chest. I sniff the autumn air and his warm fur and the heaps of fallen leaves.

When Mum's done with the bannock, I mix up the fudge we call rocket fuel. I melt butter, peanut butter and chocolate chips and stir in dried berries and icing sugar. I give the pot to Rachel to lick.

"They need more chocolate," says Rachel.

"Forget it," I tell her. Rachel always wants more chocolate.

That night, I lie in bed and think about Dad's new medicine and Mum thinking we're better off without him. It seems to me that sometimes when he's thinking about animals or where we're going, he just forgets about being depressed.

Then I hear scratching sounds coming from the tree where Ginger's tied.

Oh, no, I think. A few days before a dog has pups, she often starts digging nests for them.

6

DURING THE night, something wakens me from a dream about running dogs alone in the night.

Dad is cross-legged on the edge of the caribou hide, fishing in his pack by candlelight. His shadow is huge on the canvas wall.

"What are you doing?" asks Mum softly. I lie very still so they won't know I'm listening.

"Looking for aspirin."

"They're in the sled bag. What's wrong?"

Dad pulls on his moccasins and opens the stove drafts. The wood catches. I see the red coals through the hole.

"I've got a headache," he says. He lifts the coffee pot onto the back of the stove. "I'm sorry. I know I'm not good company."

"You don't talk to me. I'm tired of having to guess what you're thinking."

Dad rolls a cigarette and lights it. Before he got depressed, he never smoked inside.

"I can't talk," he says. "A door keeps closing inside me. I can't keep it open. And I'm alone on the other side."

Mum is quiet for so long that I think she's fallen back asleep. I'm not sure what he's talking about. It's felt to me like he isn't really there anymore. Is that how it feels to him, too?

"I don't understand," Mum says finally. "You're not alone. You have us."

Dad draws on his cigarette. I see the red end glowing in the darkness. He butts it out on the tobacco can lid.

"I can't explain," he says. He flicks the butt through the stove draft. "It's like a nightmare but I don't wake up. I can't see any future. None."

"But I love you," says Mum, so quietly I can hardly make out the words.

They used to end every day with tea around the stove and Mum telling Dad about whatever she was carving. It used to bother me sometimes because I felt they could be happy just with each other. Now I'd love to see them that way.

"Even if I do get better," says Dad, "what am I going to do with myself? There's no money left in trapping and I don't know how to do anything else."

He ducks through the tent opening. His voice sounded like he was crying. A thin wedge of stars and northern lights shimmer between the canvas flaps.

Every serious dog racer has a handler. Dad promised the first time I told him that I wanted to race that he would be mine. Handlers and mushers have to talk all the time. They talk about dogs and trails and weather and gear. Handlers help make dog beds and feed dogs and make sure the musher gets rest at the checkpoints. Dad will be there for me whenever I pull off the trail. Even the dogs will relax when they know he's there.

I wait a long time listening for Dad to come back. Finally, I fall asleep.

•••

When I wake next, I get out of my bag and light the stove. I mix up the morning bannock of water, flour, milk powder, baking powder and salt. While the stove's heating, I get up my nerve to go outside and check Ginger.

The morning is clear and cold. Ginger is asleep in her nest, round as ever. I let out a breath I didn't know I was holding. I let her sleep and turn to Pepper instead. I rub along his spine, and he knocks me down in the snow and licks me.

"Salt," I call. Salt runs away from me to the end of his chain. How is he going to learn to work properly if he doesn't trust me? I squat down in the snow so I'm at his eye level.

"Come on, Salt."

Salt looks down his long nose at me.

"It's okay, boy," I say very softly. "Good dog!" I stand and walk steadily toward him, holding out my bare hand for him to sniff. Then I scratch gently behind his ears.

Salt lowers his head and pushes slightly toward me.

"Good dog." I squat down beside him again and mutter to him for a few minutes about what a wonderful dog he is and how he's going to love pulling. I'm not sure he's convinced but he does move in closer, his ears pricked and his tail unfolded from between his legs.

Finally, I take the coffee pot to look for water. I walk along the creek until I hear it running. Then I whack the ice with my ax a couple of times and listen again. I try three different spots before I see water running under where I've chopped. I bang again and the water seeps into the hole and fills it up like a basin. I chop the hole wide enough to scoop in the pot and turn back to the tent.

Bunches of willows are spread across the valley. Ptarmigan are rushing around, leaving scratch marks on top of the snow. They're mostly still white-feathered from the winter, but their heads and foreparts have already turned brown. By the time their chicks are born, they'll be almost invisible again against the willow bark.

In early spring, they cluster in mountain passes, fighting for territory and a mate. Two males are rushing at each other right by the end of the dog sled, the female watching. They do more walking than flying this time of year. Even when the dogs chase them, they just rise in the air to the next willow clump and land again. I can almost hear the dogs wanting the birds for supper.

Mum said I was born in a good ptarmigan year. Every ten years or so the tundra turns into a chicken yard. The snow fleas are out now, black specks hopping over the snow. They appear overnight when the snow is turning to slush. Yesterday there weren't any, but this morning the snow is speckled with so many I can't use it for melt water.

"Becky?" yells Rachel.

"Coming," I sigh. Rachel's wanting me to watch her more and more. She forgets I have dogs to take care of.

I duck inside. Rachel is turning somersaults on the sleeping bags, dressed only in her underwear and socks.

"Watch this," she says and does two back-flips in a row before she bumps into the tent wall. It shakes, of course.

"Stop it," says Mum automatically. "The tent will fall down."

Mum is sitting cross-legged on the edge of the sleeping bags holding her sketch pad on her knees, her long hair falling over her face. Every few minutes she crumples up a page, looks up and tosses it in the fire.

After breakfast, I fold up the tent, dump the ashes out of the stove onto the snow and pack my sled. I hold out a bit of bannock to coax Salt over but he cringes as far away as he can get.

"I thought we were friends now," I tell him. I toss the bannock to Ginger instead. Dad hates me giving people food to the dogs, but his face has that closed look so he won't say much.

"Are you sick, Dad?" Rachel asks, bouncing over.

"I'm busy," he says, scowling. "I don't have time to talk."

Rachel climbs on top of the load into the sleeping bags, sticks her thumb in her mouth and slides the other arm around Taffy.

I go over to Rachel and hug her. She keeps herself stiff.

"Do you think Taffy wants to help me harness my dogs?" I ask.

She takes her thumb out long enough to laugh. She's got a pile of books stuck down in the sleeping bag. She likes to read if the sun gets hot enough for her to turn the pages without freezing her hands. Rachel is such a chatterbox that I forget she's smart. She taught herself to read when Mum was teaching me in correspondence school.

Mum is already breaking trail. We're supposed to catch up when the dogs are harnessed. Ginger looks surprised when I slip the harness over her head. Pepper screams cheerfully and jumps on his back legs, and Salt tries to hide on the far side of the tree.

"Come on, Salt," I coax again.

He squeals as if I've hurt him.

"Enough of that." I drag him over to the traces. "I want to be friends with you," I snap between gritted teeth. He stands with his tail between his legs while I feed the harness over his head. Then he lies down so I can't place the straps behind his front legs. I haul him to his feet. He whimpers and curls up in a ball.

I hate it when Salt acts like he's scared of me.

"Catch," says Rachel. She throws a strip of jerky from the sled bag and I feed it to Salt.

"Good dog," I coax, patting his nose. I'm amazed when Salt stands and allows me to finish pulling on the harness. His gray face looks cute and eager. His tail emerges for once and wags.

"Sit!" I tell him. Salt sits and looks directly at me for the first time. I toss him the other half of the jerky. When did he ever learn to sit? Someone must have spent time with him somewhere. I ruffle his fur before he has time to back away.

"Let's go," I shout to Ginger. My toboggan breaks out as the dogs throw themselves forwards in their traces. I catch hold of the handlebars as they fly by and hop on.

•••

Later in the morning, the creek we've been following heads up between two peaks, so Mum veers off from it straight across the pass. Every minute we can travel before the sun gets too hot counts, because there are no more willows even for firewood. We can't make camp until we get to the next creek on the far side of the pass and start heading down.

At first my dogs keep going, but the pass between the creeks is filled with soft, deep drifts of snow. The sun is reflecting off the snow with no trees to break the glare. I feel sick for Ginger having to work so hard when she's hot.

With a whimper, Salt looks back at me, digs in his paws and stops. He lies down in his traces and curls up. Pepper jumps up and down in his harness and whines to get going, but the two front dogs can't drag Salt in the deep wet snow. Ginger tugs a few times and then stands still.

"Let's go," I yell. Dad is right behind and I know he's watching. My heart feels like I've been running uphill. Someone has spent time training this dog, I tell myself. He does know what he's doing. "Salt," I shout. "Let's go!"

Salt stays curled up. It's not fair to Ginger when he won't move. She has to work harder to break the toboggan out again. Besides, Salt has to learn I'm in charge. A dog team is like a wolf pack, Dad told me once. The dogs think of the musher as the dominant wolf in their packs.

This has gone on long enough. I walk around beside Salt, making myself as big as possible. I stand over him, up to my thighs in soft snow, and yank him to his feet. Then I yell louder than I've ever yelled in my life.

"I said, let's go!" I yell it right into his ear. Startled, Salt screams, lurches forward and runs. The toboggan breaks out and I barely manage to catch the back of my sled as it whizzes by. I jog for a bit, hanging onto the handlebars. The dogs' traces are tight, and the hot, spring mountain wind flies against my face. I don't think about Dad or what will become of Ginger's pups or anything else.

I ride a bit, then kick, then ride again, my team yipping merrily. From behind, Rachel begins to sing.

"Good dogs!" I shout. Their fur is shining in the sun. "Good dogs!"

•••

For about a mile we mush like that without me having to push at all. Now that my own team is working better, Dad's dogs are right behind. A couple of times Egypt actually bumps into me, stepping on my heels. It makes me trip and breaks the rhythm of running behind my sled.

"Whoa," I shout finally and jump on my brake. Pepper leaps up, trying to keep the sled moving, but Salt slinks a glance back at me and then curls up.

"Good dogs," I call. Then I look back. "Dad, I'm going to untie your dogs from my toboggan. Egypt will follow now without it. She keeps running into my heels."

He's standing on the back of his sled with his head down. "She won't go then. She'll just stop."

"She'll do it."

He looks over my shoulder as if he can't see me.

"Please."

"Do what you want. Just go."

I untie Egypt. With her bumping into me, I'll get tired much faster, and I might have to push my sled again later when the snow gets even softer.

The sun gets higher and higher and the ptarmigan are cackling madly. They are almost impossible to spot against the white glare of the sun.

"Ack, ack, ack, ack," Rachel yells at two males who are rushing at each other on our left. Taffy pokes her head out of the sleeping bag, spits and tries to leap out after them.

"Get back," Rachel shouts and grabs the cat just in time.

I'm looking back over my shoulder to see what she's doing, and my sled almost tips over because I'm not concentrating.

"Can't you keep your cat in the sled?" I snap.

"I am," she shouts back. She sticks her thumb back in her mouth and I turn back to watch my dogs.

Mum is way ahead, and I push for awhile trying to catch up, the sun hot on my left cheek and the breeze warm from the south. A caterpillar, fuzzy as Pepper, wiggles across the snow. I point it out to Rachel, who scoops it up. Every little while I take the map from my sled bag and compare what I'm seeing around me to its contours. I have to ride while I do this, and Salt looks back and whines every time, but he doesn't lie down.

The map makes sense this trip! Mum and Dad have pointed out where we are on maps for years, but I've never been able to follow the route myself.

When the sun is overhead, Mum calls a break.

"There's no time," says Dad. "We have to get over to the next creek where there's wood. We can't even melt snow for drinking water here."

"I want to stop," says Mum. "The girls need to eat and the dogs are overheating. If we push them much further, they'll give out."

The dogs are panting. When we stop, both teams lie on their sides, then roll in the snow to cool off.

Dad doesn't talk. He walks back a few steps along the trail and stands by himself. I get out the tea and jerky and rocket fuel that I made last night. Rachel hops off the sled to release her caterpillar far away from Taffy, and collapses on her back to make angels in the snow. I fold the sleeping bag over Taffy so she won't run off after ptarmigan. Rachel should think of this herself, but she doesn't.

"Your cat's going to run off," I mutter. "You should watch her."

Mum tickles Rachel with her feet and Rachel rolls over and over like the dogs.

"Do you know where we are?" she asks between rolls.

"You've sure got lots of energy," Mum tells her. "And Becky's right. Watch your cat, please."

I take the map from my sled bag and unfold it.

"Look," I tell her, pointing to the mountain across from us. "See that peak?" I point on the map. "In another mile we'll start heading down."

Mum looks back and forth at us, smiling. Rachel and I don't always get along. In fact, until Dad got depressed, Mum and Dad were always saying how sick they were of us fighting.

Now Rachel doesn't seem to want to fight with me anymore. Maybe she's trying to make Dad happy, too.

"Good rocket fuel," Mum says.

Rachel named our daily fudge mixture rocket fuel because the balls give her so much energy. We take turns mixing it up in the tent at night. Dad used to make pemmican balls and they're the very best of all — dried, powdered caribou meat with brown sugar and peanut butter and cranberries and spices. He wouldn't ever tell us what spices but he did say that if we ate more than a couple, our stomachs would hurt from the food swelling.

It's been a long time since Dad made them, though.

Dad turns around and I see in the glare of the sun how really thin he's become. I check his mood by watching his face these days. It looks different, older, the bones sharper and his eyes bigger. The corners sag down. I look away and remember a trip Dad and I took around the trap-line once.

"The thing about running dogs," Dad says, poking a stick in the campfire flames, "is that you have to believe in yourself and your dogs. You have to believe that your dogs won't let you down, will do what you ask them to do. And that's why you have to think carefully about what you ask them."

Away from the light of the flames the forest is starlit and shadowed. Bear's eyes glint in the dark. The other dogs are curled on their spruce bough beds, heads tucked under tails. Far above us, wisps of aurora flicker above the mountain ridges and the moonlit ice. Bear stares at us and whines deep in his throat.

"Never ask a dog to do something that you don't think he can do."

I leave the warmth of the fire and bury my face in Bear's neck. I stand and rub along the length of his spine and Bear presses against me. The sky is enormous and beautiful.

Dad throws an armful of boughs on the fire, and they spark and dance into the deep, domed sky.

"Are you ready yet?" Dad asks. Mum harnesses her snowshoes back up and Rachel grabs the last of the rocket fuel and clambers into the sled bag.

"I thought you said there wasn't enough chocolate in them," I say.

"Really?" asks Rachel. "Did I say that?"

I shake my head. Rachel claims to never remember the irritating things she says. Too bad I remember them all!

Again, I don't go behind the sled to tell the dogs to go. I haul Salt to a standing position, yell in his ear and then jump on when he bolts and the sled flies by. Whenever he tries to skid to a stop, I run alongside him and yell and he keeps going, whining all the time like someone's beating him. I feel bad about yelling at him, but it's easier on Ginger when he pulls.

Later I see the next valley spread out below, with the Snake River winding between bluffs and the mountains unfolding to the north up toward our cabin. Mum is so exhausted that she stops every so often to rest on one knee in the snow. You can't sit down in snowshoes any other way because they're so wide.

Our cabin is twenty miles farther up the bank of the river. The last time I saw it was before Dad got sick a year ago. It was home then but it's been so long and so much has happened that I don't know if it will feel like home ever again. If Dad isn't living with us, I won't want to come back here. How could Mum think that it would be best? Does she think life will go on just the same except without him?

I'm so tired that even my arms hurt. I'd like to ride, but I know the dogs are too tired to pull me. Ginger should be in a warm house filled with straw, not pulling in harness. I shouldn't have brought her here.

I keep pushing on the handlebars. The heat has sapped the dogs' energy. Somehow seeing our river makes me want to cry. It reminds me of when Dad wasn't depressed. I want my dad back.

When we finally make it down to the willows where we can camp, it's already dark. Dad throws up the tent while Mum gets firewood. Rachel claims to be cold and Mum lets her sit by a bonfire while everyone else works. I unharness the dogs and unpack both sleds. My dogs will have to sleep without spruce boughs tonight because I don't have the energy to chop any.

Then Ginger sticks her nose into the palm of my hand and nuzzles against me. It's hard to believe she was so timid when I got her, that she wouldn't even step off the roof of her doghouse to meet me.

Rachel walks over and snaps off dead brush.

"Can you get enough for the morning kindling?" I ask.

"No problem," says Rachel, as if she was thinking of it all along.

"Rachel?" I ask.

"Yeah?"

"See if some of the green boughs will snap off, too. Maybe you can do it without the ax."

Rachel stands on tiptoes and breaks off several boughs.

"It's easy," she says. "Want me to make your dog beds?"

"Thanks," I say. "I'd love it."

Supper is leftover bannock and jerky. Mum mixes up chocolate and dried berries for rocket fuel without even cooking it. I throw a piece of jerky out to Ginger when no one's looking. She gobbles it down and whines. Then she starts digging again, and I force myself to leave the warm tent and throw down the sled bag from my toboggan for her. No one notices. They're all tired, too.

We get into our sleeping bags as soon as we've finished eating. Mum doesn't say anything. Maybe she doesn't want to believe what she's seeing with Ginger. Or maybe she's waiting for me to tell her.

My muscles are so sore that it's hard to get to sleep. I turn over and over and sometimes I look at Dad and he's just lying there, his arms under his head, staring up at the tent wall without moving a single muscle in his face. His eyes are wide open.

Maybe you can't sleep much when you're depressed. Maybe he dreams about Bear, too.

"Dad," I whisper once. He doesn't answer but something ripples across his face. It looks like he's trying not to cry.

From the forest comes the hoot of a great horned owl — five short hoots and a long one at the end. Another owl answers through the night and the two call back and forth while the moonlight throws shadows along the tent walls.

If we love Dad enough, I think, it will make him better. I decide I'll help out even more tomorrow.

Outside, Ginger is restless. She whines and scratches awhile, then whines again.

Will her pups even live if they're born in the cold like that? I've heard of mushers finding frozen puppies in the morning. It's warm enough while the sun is up in the day but as soon as it's gone, winter comes back for the night.

Suddenly, I make up my mind.

"Ginger's not feeling good," I say in the dark tent.

Dad doesn't answer and Mum's asleep.

"She worked too hard today," I say. "I'm bringing her in." Then I throw off my sleeping bag and do it before Dad has a chance to say no.

Ginger leans against me when I go to unsnap her chain. She follows me in quietly and curls into my side, Salt whining as he watches her leave. I don't know if Dad even heard. Logs settle slowly in the stove and finally burn out before I'm able to fall asleep.

7

IN THE morning, I manage to get Ginger out of the tent and tied back up before anybody wakes up. Anybody except Salt and Pepper, I mean. Salt actually stands and barks, he's so glad to see Ginger return. Pepper rushes around his willow in mad circles tangling himself up, burying his nose in the snow and sending it flying. It takes a few minutes to get him untangled because whenever I come near, he charges at me like a friendly bull.

I like the feeling of being awake alone and watching the coffee pot boil on my fire. I like watching the sunshine touching first on the mountain peaks, then slowly spreading down their sides.

After the morning bannock, Rachel and Mum load gear on the toboggans while Dad takes down the tent. I notice Rachel doesn't even have to be asked to help. Dad carries the still-burning stove out with thick mitts, dumps coals in the snow and packs the pipes inside the woodbox when they're cool. I harness dogs and tie up my load.

At first we follow the creek down to the river from the pass. Salt pulls forward — maybe because it's downhill and he's scared of the toboggan bumping into him or maybe because he's finally learned.

"Good dog," I call to him.

I saved part of my breakfast bannock for rewards. Every half-hour or so I stop and feed each dog a bit.

We run the dogs right on the creek ice, which has overflowed and then refrozen so there is only a skiff of snow over the new ice. There's just enough snow that the dogs don't slide, and Mum doesn't have to wear her snowshoes. The dogs don't need me to push at all. They even seem to step higher now, light and happy, skimming over the creek. At first I run. Then when I get too tired to keep up I hop on, singing snatches of songs with Rachel whistling from her nest. My dogs don't even slow for a minute.

We make camp as soon as we get to the river. There is lots of dead spruce for firewood, and the ice is tramped down bank to bank with caribou tracks. Over top of their tracks are the prints of wolves following close behind. There are tangles of willow lining the river with snowshoe rabbit trails around them. There's always so much more life along the big rivers.

The side straps on a couple of the dog harnesses are starting to tear. Mum is outside in the sunshine sewing them, and Rachel is drawing in her journal.

"Can you come and draw with me?" Rachel asks Mum.

"Can't," says Mum. "There's chores to finish."

Mum has burned every sketch she's drawn on this trip. The project for the art gallery was supposed to be her big chance, but she's not even trying. She's letting her dream just slip away.

Ginger is sleeping on her spruce boughs, Salt close beside her. I'll tie him before I go to bed in case wolves come around, but for now he just wants to be near Ginger. Pepper is beating up a willow, growling and snapping at the flailing branches.

Dad's sitting outside on a stump, as usual, head down. I take a ball of snare wire out of the sled bag and cut it into lengths with the wire cutters.

This time I'm going to do it. I'm going to make Dad talk to me.

"Dad," I say.

"Yes."

"I'm going to set some rabbit snares. Will you come?"

Dad opens his mouth and closes it. He starts to shake his head.

"Please."

He grins and, for a moment, the grin reaches his eyes and his face clears.

"Okay," he says, and pats his pocket to make sure there's tobacco. It's hard to believe that he'd decided to quit before he got sick.

"Can I come?" Rachel yells from inside the tent. Through the open flap I can see her practicing handstands, with Taffy crouched ready to attack at the end of the bag. Smoke curls out of the stovepipe and through the trees.

Mum will have a fit when she realizes what Rachel is doing in there. It's dangerous to fool around in the tent with the fire going. Still, Rachel must get bored sitting on top of that toboggan load all day.

"Sorry," I tell her. "But you can show me your journal when we get back. And you should quit the handstands."

Dad and I walk out on the river ice. I hear my dogs howling behind us. They're sad that I've gone without them! The sun is going down behind the mountains to the west, and long shadows slant across the snow. We stoop to check out the caribou tracks. Dad's rifle is slung over one shoulder.

Before we left town for this trip, Dad spent most of his days lying on the couch and not speaking. At least he looks more normal now.

He takes off his glove and brushes the frost from a track.

"Yesterday's, I think," he says.

These caribou are heading north toward our cabin and up to their calving grounds. About thirty miles upriver a creek flows in from a pass high up in the mountains. The cows will be heading up there soon to calve. Only barrenland caribou migrate long distances up to the Arctic. The herd here is woodland caribou and they have their own local calving ground that they use year after year. We've come across cows giving birth on ridge-tops in the middle of the spring night, storm clouds swirling above their heads. Dad says they give birth up high to get away from wolves. Mum says more likely it's to get away from mosquitoes.

I don't want to waste this time alone with Dad. I've noticed when he's talking about animals he seems the most normal. At least he says something.

"Would you take a caribou now if we saw one?" I ask, just to get him started.

He looks up at me. He's having a good day. Both teams are working better. The snow is holding out.

"Hunting season is over. You know that," he says.

"When we get to the cabin, can we go checking around for caribou kill?" Once we found a caribou that had dropped in the freezing river when the wolves had killed it. I guess they hadn't been able to get it out. The meat smelled and tasted perfectly fresh.

It's hard to explain the difference between wild and storebought meat. Wild meat has more taste. It's like crunching fresh garden carrots instead of the ones shipped up to the store from down south.

"We'll see when we get there," says Dad. "Come on. It's getting late. I thought you wanted to set some snares."

This is the time. He's feeling good enough to answer my questions. He's not like this very often.

We climb the bank and enter the willows. There are snowshoe rabbit trails everywhere. They are actually hares, and their big paws make trails like snowshoes over the snow's surface. When we find where a trail narrows between willows, we set a wire loop anchored to a stick by the side of a trail. The rabbit should poke its head through the loop when it hops along the trail tonight.

I finish wiring my first loop to a stick. The loop hangs about a foot off the snow, over where the rabbit will hop. The snare should fasten around the rabbit's neck and kill it at once.

A kid in town told me this was cruel, but it feels different when you've been raised in the woods. All of nature, Dad told me once, is busy eating another part of nature. He said he likes things to be killed with as little suffering as possible and he never takes more than he needs. Maybe you have to grow up with wolves and caribou as neighbors to understand. If I were an animal I'd rather live a free life until I was killed quickly, than spend my life in a box or a pen.

I find four more good rabbit trails, twist the wire into loops and anchor them to their guide sticks. The last sun is shining through a low pass here onto my face.

"Dad?" I ask, before I can change my mind.

Dad is standing to one side waiting for me to finish with the rabbit run. He's not even helping, just picking frozen highbush cranberries and eating them.

He looks over at me and pops a berry in his mouth.

"Are you trying to say something?" he asks.

"I don't know what's going on with you," I get out, finally.

"What are you talking about?"

"Mum told me your brain is sick. I don't understand it."

His face tightens and he steps back from the berry bush.

"Sometimes you don't talk to us for days. It's like you're not even there. But then you're normal, like now." I don't know how to say any of this to him. I'm not even sure what I'm asking. But I am sure that I need him to talk about it.

"What don't you understand?"

I feel my face flushing. I'm getting mad. I'm sick of trying to please him when it doesn't make any difference.

"What's wrong with you? If your brain is sick, what's wrong with it? And why can't you fix it?"

For a long minute he doesn't answer, and I'm sure he's going to walk away. And I decide that if he does, I'm going to follow him and keep asking.

Then he walks over to a log, brushes the snow off it and sits down. He takes his tobacco and his papers from his pocket, taps tobacco onto the paper and then twists it shut. He takes a lighter from another pocket and draws on his cigarette.

I hate his smoking. He was always supposed to quit.

"I thought your mother explained it to you."

"So? I want you to explain it. Tell me why you're so different. Are you mad at me? I didn't do anything to you."

He waits another minute and I feel the cold seeping through my clothes.

"It's not your fault. I'm not mad at anyone."

"You ignore us most of the time. I hate it."

"Do you know what it's like to be depressed?"

"Yes. Mum told me. You're sad. You can't sleep properly and you don't feel like eating…" I try to remember what else Mum has said.

"Did you ever feel like you were in a fog? Maybe when you had the flu with a fever?"

"I guess so." But I'm not mean to people when I'm sick.

"That's part of it. Sometimes I'm in a fog so thick that I don't feel anything and I can't think properly or even remember things." He tosses the cigarette to the ground and grinds it under his boot. "Those must be the times when it feels to you like I'm not really there."

"Will it ever stop?" I'm scared to ask.

"Sometimes, like today, the fog blows away and I can see you and the rest of the world around me just like normal."

From across the frozen river, I hear the smack of the ax. Mum must be splitting more wood.

"I can't help it." He's talking so low I can barely make out his words. "I can't make the fog lift."

"But I'm doing all the things you've always wanted me to do and you don't even notice. I'm even training my own team."

"Maybe you could tell me about it later," Dad says quietly. "Or you could even write it all down."

I know he doesn't like talking about it but I've waited so long without asking him that my words come tumbling out.

"Will you ever care about it?"

"I hope so, Becky."

How can a father say that he hopes he will care? Before I can stop myself, tears are in my eyes.

"Are you trying to make it better?" That's what I most want to know.

"I'm taking medicine. It's supposed to help."

"Does it?"

"I'm talking to you, aren't I? The fog still comes down but it lifts sometimes now. More and more often, I think. But when it does come down, it feels like it will last forever."

That isn't what I want to hear. I want him to say that he will be fine, that he can control himself now that he knows it bothers me so much. I want to know that we will sit around the tent stove at night singing old freight-train songs like we used to. I want him to pay attention to my team, to notice how they're starting to work.

I don't want to look at his face anymore to check out his mood. He's the grown-up. I want him to watch his own moods.

More than anything, though, I want him to be like my old dad again, not like a stranger.

The sun is behind the mountains now. There are no more shadows on the snow and the temperature is dropping fast.

"I can't promise you anything. If I could make it better, believe me, I would," he says.

I go to him then and grab hold of his parka. For a minute, I stand in the cold woods holding onto him, and I don't want to ever let go.

"By the way, Becky, your dogs are running great," he says.

I actually laugh, I'm so surprised. "Did you notice that I've never had to hit them?" I ask.

"Never thought you would," he says.

It's not fair. He smells like he always has — of wood smoke and dogs. I take his hand and we walk back out on the river ice, caribou tracks from bank to bank like there have always been, and mountains ranging wild and beautiful about us. We walk back to the tent, a square of candle-lit canvas silhouetted against the dropping dark and the enormous, silent valley.

When we get closer, I see Mum standing outside with

the candle. She's staring down at Ginger, who is lying on her spruce bough bed.

Even from a distance I can see that Mum isn't pleased.

8

"BECKY," says Mum.

I walk up the bank beside Dad. He goes into the tent and I hear him lift the coffee pot off the stove and pour himself a cup. The tent shakes. There's a crashing sound — Rachel doing somersaults on the sleeping bag.

"Stop that," growls Dad. "I've told you before."

"Becky," says Mum, looking at me over her glasses.

"Yes."

"Could you come here."

Slowly I walk over to the white mound — Ginger. She lumbers to her feet and pokes her muzzle into my hand. I don't even have to call her anymore.

"This dog is pregnant. You must have known that before we left town."

"I couldn't leave her, Mum. She's just starting to trust me."

"Why did you bring her on a trip like this when she's going to have pups? She shouldn't be pulling."

"I know. That's why I've been pushing so hard on the handlebars when it's been rough."

"Who's the father of the puppies?"

"I don't know. She must have got pregnant right when I got her."

There's a long silence. Finally, Mum reaches down and scratches Ginger behind the ears.

"You didn't think," she says. "I thought you were responsible enough to have your own team."

"I am responsible. I've taken good care of them." I feel sick. What if she won't let me keep the puppies? And how can she talk about trust anyhow? She's the one who wants Dad to live by himself just because he's sick. I trusted her to keep our family together. I trusted them both.

"You should have told me." Mum doesn't even look mad. She just looks tired. "What's going to happen when we go back to town? We'll only to be able to take what we can fit into packs for us and for the dogs."

"Puppies can walk when they're only a few weeks old."

"It would take weeks to walk out with a litter of pups waddling along behind us."

"Then I'll carry them."

"You only have two arms. Why didn't you tell me about this before we left town?"

How can I explain to her? I need to breed my own

line of racing dogs. I need a couple of generations, and Ginger's pups are the beginning.

This all flashes through my mind, but I don't say any of it. I just stand there. The truth is that I didn't think about what would happen to the pups. I wanted them with me, and I didn't feel like talking to Mum about it. Of course I can't tell her that or she'd want to know why. Mum's a great believer in talking problems out with the people you're close to. The trouble is that I don't feel close to Mum anymore. I don't feel close to anyone — except maybe my dogs.

If I can't have my family together, then at least I'll have my dogs.

"Are you going to tell Dad?" I ask.

"That's your job," she says, and she walks into the tent.

For a long time I stay outside, digging through the snow to bare dirt and moss, looking for cranberries still fresh after the winter.

There aren't any.

That night Dad seems almost normal. He says a couple of things without being even asked, and when Rachel does a back flip and knocks over his coffee, he just tells her to go flip outside.

"In the snow?" asks Rachel, horrified.

"In the snow," says Dad, with a sound almost like a laugh.

"Come with me, Becky."

It sounds easier than staying in the tent with Mum.

Outside, I sit and watch Rachel go through her routine. Taffy sits in the doorway of the tent licking her paws. Pepper hurls himself against his chain frantically, hoping to eat her, I guess.

Whenever Rachel does a handstand, I can't help smiling. She just looks so happy.

"Let me try," I tell her. I practice over and over but there's always a moment when I know I've lost my balance and I sprawl face first in the snow.

"Don't lean so far forwards," Rachel tells me and chucks a snowball at Pepper. He leaps on it and eats the snow.

Mum boils grain and meat scraps in the pot hanging from the tripod outside, adds dry dog food and oil and feeds both teams. I notice that she gives an extra helping to Ginger.

I don't even offer to help her. I don't want to be near her right now. I keep trying to figure out how those pups can get to town. Will Dad even let me keep them? Once he told me that it's kinder to kill pups at birth if nobody wants them. He shot Bear and he loved him. How much would it bother him to get rid of newborn pups?

•••

Eventually Mum goes inside and even Rachel gets cold and wants to go to bed. Mum doesn't say anything to

Dad. I'm beginning to wish she would so I could get it over with. All the time, I'm feeling worse and worse. Ginger should be inside, too, but I can't bring her in until I've told Dad.

Finally, everybody else gets in their sleeping bags and Mum calls me in.

"Dad," I say when the candle has been blown out and nobody has spoken for a while. I'm hoping everyone else is sleeping.

"What?"

I can tell by his voice that he's remembering all the questions I asked him when we were rabbit snaring. I know he's afraid I'm going to ask him more questions.

"Dad. I have to tell you something."

"What?" asks Rachel.

I ignore her. "Dad. Ginger's having pups."

"Hurray!" shouts Rachel, sitting up in her bag.

Dad doesn't answer.

"Did you hear me, Dad?" I ask.

"I heard you."

"Well. Do you mind?"

"Of course I mind. How do you think we're going to get them back to town?"

"I'll take care of that."

"How?"

I can't answer. Rachel has the good sense to lie back down and be quiet.

"When are the pups going to be born?" Dad asks at last.

"Any day."

There's another long silence. I can hear Rachel cuddling up to Taffy, who's purring steadily.

"You can't keep them," says Dad. "You know that, don't you?"

"I have to keep them."

"I don't want to talk about it."

I won't listen to this. "Can I bring her in?" I ask. "She's probably uncomfortable out there in the snow."

Dad's quiet for so long that I think he hasn't heard me.

"I suppose so," he says at last.

I slip on my boots and go out to Ginger. The moon is out and the northern lights are opening and closing like fiery curtains across the starry sky.

I've done it. I've told them but it doesn't sound like either Mum or Dad want my pups to live long enough to open their eyes.

A strong gust of wind blows through the surrounding spruce trees. Ice cracks like a gunshot. I close my eyes, remembering Bear.

I know one thing. Those puppies are mine. And they're going to grow up and run races and have a great life. They will be the start of my racing team.

"Come on, Ginger," I say, letting her free. She licks my hand, and her lips curl up like she's smiling.

Then she follows me into the tent.

9

ALL NIGHT I lie awake in my sleeping bag trying not to think about what's going to happen to the pups. Dad, for once, seems to sleep, and I even hear him snore — something I haven't heard in a long time. During the night, gusts of wind begin to scream from the south. The tent walls slam in and out with each gust and I hear the dogs whimper and scratch at their snow burrows. Once, Ginger lifts her head and puts her nose on my arm, her eyes shining in the moonlight. I pat her for a few minutes, and it makes me feel a little better.

When the first light seeps in, I light the fire and stoop through the tent flap. A flock of white birds swoops through the sky, landing on a willow close by. Snow buntings, the first migratory birds I've noticed this spring. The sun bursts over the mountains, and I can feel its heat instantly. The buntings sing, and their song is like water trickling through the muskeg and the moss.

"Come on, Ginger," I whisper. She slinks out of the tent and follows me across the river to check the rabbit snares. I don't know how I'm going to keep the puppies yet, but I'm going to do it. As for Ginger, I want her to be my friend as well as a working dog. What's the point of having a dog team if you don't love your dogs?

Ginger follows right on my heels on yesterday's trail. Her coat shines white in the sunlight.

The last two snares hold rabbits.

"Don't worry, Ginger," I tell her, when she tries to sniff them. "I'll boil some for you later. The meat will be good for your pups." Ginger whines as if she understands.

Back at the tent, I chain her back up for awhile and give the rabbits to Mum.

"Great," she says. "Fresh meat for supper." Dad and Mum are drinking coffee while the bannock fries. Rachel is doing stretches on the bags. I pour hot water from a pot on the stove and mix up cocoa for us. The wind is gusting louder and louder.

"It feels like a chinook," says Mum, standing in the open flaps of the tent. "Wind's actually warm." Snow slides off the tent roof. "I don't think we're going anywhere today. The snow's melting."

"I'll go scout ahead on the river," says Dad. "It's too warm for the dogs but I can break some trail. I'll be back tonight."

"Could I come?" I ask. I don't want to be with Mum on our own. The day feels very long if we're not going anywhere.

"No," says Dad. "I've got a headache. Okay?"

I nod. Mum will want to talk about things and I don't want to.

Dad's looking right at me. "It's better if I keep busy," he says, like I'm a grown-up.

What about me? I feel better when I'm busy, too.

"Sure, Dad," I say. "No problem."

After breakfast, Dad grabs his snowshoes and heads off down the river. Mum gets out her sketchbook and tries to draw. I take the ax and begin chopping spruce boughs off the trees when I notice Dad's tobacco can sitting under the tree. He must have forgotten it.

I chop a heap of boughs for Ginger and then another heap that I spread out in front of the tent. I try one handstand and this time I teeter over and fall on my back. It's a step up from falling on my face, I guess.

"I've got something to show you," I tell Rachel. "Come here."

"What is it?" she asks, coming out.

"An exercise pad so you can practice."

"Hurray!" shouts Rachel, jumping on it. She tugs off her boots and starts rolling, then somersaulting backwards. "Thanks," she shouts between rolls.

"That was nice of you," Mum says from the tent. Her voice isn't so much sad as it's flat, like she's somehow become older and tired.

I go in and sit beside her. She's sitting on the edge of

the sleeping bags with scrunched-up pieces of paper heaped around her.

"Nothing seems to work for me these days," she says, her curls tucked behind her ears like Rachel's. She's drawing the riverbank in pencil with the water pooling on top of the ice. "You're mad at me, Becky."

A gust of wind shakes the tent walls, and Mum's pencil wavers. She scrunches up the paper, tosses the paper balls in the stove and tries again.

Suddenly, I'm so angry I can hardly talk. I take a few deep breaths to see if I can calm down and then I don't care anymore.

"It's you," I start.

Mum pushes her glasses back and looks up from her drawing. "Me?"

"I heard you, Mum. I heard you talking on the phone before we left town. You were telling someone that Dad would be better off by himself."

"Why didn't you tell me?"

"Why should I? You weren't talking to me. You said Rachel and I would be better off without him."

"Why are you mad then? Because I said it, or because it might be true?"

I feel something growing in my throat. My throat feels like I'm choking. I can barely speak and all the time the wind is screaming around the tent and Rachel is laughing outside on her spruce bough exercise mat.

"I'm not a quitter," I yell. "When someone trusts me,

I don't let them down. You do. And now you expect me to let Ginger down, too."

Mum reaches out a hand and puts it on my arm but I shrug her off. I can see there are tears in her eyes but I don't care.

"I'm sorry, Becky. I'm doing my best."

I burst out of the tent. Her best! She's the grown-up. She can change things. It's just that she won't.

I walk over to Ginger, kneel in the slush and throw my arms around her neck. Ginger whines deep in her throat and pushes her nose against me. At least my dogs like me now. Things will be better with Dad when he's helping me train the puppies.

After a long time, I look up. Way down the river, a speck is getting bigger.

"Rachel," I say. "Dad's coming back. Want to walk down to meet him?"

"Okay," says Rachel, slipping on her boots. "Mum," she calls, "I'm going down with Becky to meet Dad. We can see him on the trail."

Mum murmurs something that I can't hear, and Rachel bounces over to me and takes my hand. I remember to grab Dad's tobacco. The snow is so soft that it actually clumps together for snowballs. That hardly ever happens in the north, because there isn't enough moisture.

"Hi, girls," says Dad when we catch up with him.

Rachel pats a snowball together and flies it right at

his stomach. He smiles but the smile doesn't reach his eyes. And he doesn't chuck one back like he would usually have done.

The sun is so hot that I'm sweating even without a coat. The snow is very bright and falling in sheets off the cut-banks and the trees. A mosquito flies by my nose.

"It's melting," says Dad. "Break-up is coming. The dogs won't be able to pull."

"I brought your tobacco," I tell him. "You forgot it."

Dad is carrying his hat. In the glare of the sunshine, he looks older.

"Thanks," he says, and walks on.

Back at the tent, Mum is still surrounded by piled-up bits of paper.

"Hi, Becky." She looks directly at me. Her smile does reach her eyes. I'm not mad anymore, I realize, but things aren't better, either.

"You're back quickly," she says to Dad.

He sits down and pours himself a cup of coffee. He doesn't ask Mum if she'd like one.

"The river's going," he says. "There's a channel opening about a mile upriver. It's still bridged but I don't know how long it will stay that way in this heat."

"Can't we get around it?" I ask. "Can't we go through the woods?"

"Not there," says Dad. "Cliffs come down on both sides. We'd never get the dogs around the cliffs in slush like that. We'd have to carry the toboggans and gear up the cliffs."

"We'll go tonight then," says Mum. "We'll wait until the sun goes down and it freezes so we can travel."

It's like an oven in the tent with the sun shining. The wind has died down and all I feel is hot.

"Can you be ready to travel tonight?" Dad asks.

"Sure," says Mum. She puts her blank sketching pad carefully back in its box.

•••

I help Dad collapse and fold the tent, then pack up my sled. Rachel carries the sleeping bags. She moves slowly, like she's almost asleep.

"Lie down on the toboggan," I say.

"Okay," says Rachel. She clambers up, Taffy under one arm.

It's dusky out. This time of spring, twilight lasts for hours before it gets briefly dark.

Mum tucks Rachel properly into the sled bag. She's already asleep, her thumb in her mouth, her hair in curls over her cheeks. She's done a lot of rolls and flips today.

"Do you want a hand with your dogs?" Mum asks me.

"Do you think it's safe for Ginger if I put her in harness?"

"Let me check her," says Mum. She kneels down beside Ginger and gently moves her hands where the pups are. Suddenly, she grins. "Come here, Becky." She takes my hand and presses it into Ginger.

Under my fingers, I feel something move. A pup! I keep my fingers there until the lump's gone and then press in somewhere else. I feel a leg kicking.

This pup's alive already! It kicked me!

Ginger turns her head and licks my nose.

"Good girl," I tell her.

"These pups are really important to you, aren't they?" asks Mum.

I don't want to answer her because I'm afraid I'll cry.

"When you're ready, can I talk to you about what you heard?" says Mum. "Will you tell me when you're ready to do that?"

I nod. The puppy moves under my fingers again and suddenly I laugh. Just the feel of the moving lump makes me shiver.

"A puppy is exactly what you need now," says Mum, getting to her feet and buckling on her snowshoes. "I just wish I could figure out how you could keep at least one."

Dad's standing by, taking Egypt over to harness up. I hadn't noticed him.

"Why are you getting her hopes up?" he asks Mum. "You know what we have to do."

"I think you should harness Ginger," Mum says,

ignoring Dad, "but make sure she doesn't pull much. If you leave her loose, she might wander off onto bad ice."

"I'll walk beside her," I say. "I'll make sure she doesn't strain herself."

"It's late," says Dad. "The snow's already freezing and there's enough of a crust that the dogs will stay up on it. It's going to be a long night. Let's go."

•••

"Let's go, dogs," I sing out.

The dogs gallop down the bank, barking for the sheer joy of running, and I balance the toboggan by leaning from side to side on the handlebars until we're down on the river ice.

Dad is ahead with his team, because Egypt's following behind Mum's snowshoes with no problem now, and Dad wants to keep in front of me in case there's rotten ice to go around.

Down on the ice, I run beside Ginger with a leash attached to her collar. I find myself sprinting. I need to go fast enough that she's not pulling me, too.

When I get a chance to glance back at my other dogs, I can't help feeling proud even through my worry about Ginger and her pups. Pepper is pulling like a freight train with his back humped up. He needs to keep mouthing his bit of leather but he hasn't chewed a single harness. Salt has learned to face forwards, and now he puts his nervous energy into running, not curling up and cowering.

And I've done it all myself without hitting or kicking a dog once! These were the dogs that a musher was going to shoot! Next winter I'll have a litter of pups with good pulling blood in them to train right from birth, and Dad and I will be a team.

Dad's headlight sweeps the snow, highlighting my dogs curled sleeping on bales of hay. A campfire glows with a tin bucket suspended over the flames. Dog food bubbles away. My tea kettle is to the side boiling on some coals.

"Get some sleep, Becky," says Dad, bending over a dog and examining its front paws. "That's what handlers are for — to make sure mushers get some rest during the layover."

The dogs slow a bit eventually, but I still have to trot. We keep heading down the river. Now spring meltwater is pooling on top of the ice. We come to the ice-bridge Dad mentioned. The open river is smashing against both sides of a narrow, raised strip of ice.

We stop the teams. Dad was right. There is no way around. Only across the bridge.

"It's too dangerous," says Mum. "It's not worth the risk."

"I'm going to check it out first," says Dad. He grabs a

spruce pole he's had stashed on his sled bag and takes a step onto the bridge. He stops and thumps the ice ahead of him from side to side, listening all the while for the boom of hollow ice. Carefully, he takes another step and jabs the pole, then another until he's over. All the time I hear water crashing against the ice and the dogs watching Dad and whining.

Finally he returns. "If we don't cross, we'll never make it to the cabin tonight," he says. "We'll probably never make it at all."

Bits of ice cave off the sides of the bridge and get sucked under.

Mum nods, her face tight as she ties a long rope to Egypt's collar. Then she plunks Rachel on top of the sled bag so she can pull her to safety quickly if the toboggan gets swept away, and tosses the other end of the rope ahead to Dad.

When I cross, Ginger might turn around halfway and try to head back to me and step onto thin ice.

"Becky!" Mum calls, when they're on the other side. "Catch!"

I hold out my arms as Mum tosses the coiled rope. It lands by my toboggan and I tie it to Ginger's collar. Water crashes against the ice, black and deep.

Dad tucks Rachel back into the sleeping bag and holds the other end of the rope.

"It's safe as long as you stay on the trail," he says.

I follow my toboggan, trying to put my feet down

lightly. It makes me dizzy to look down at the open water raging on both sides. A person — or a whole dog team — could get sucked into the current in no time.

Halfway over, Ginger stops. Salt and Pepper wait quietly behind her.

I have to say it properly. I have to sound firm, and not nervous.

"Let's go," I call out.

Ginger leans into her traces and pulls. The toboggan slides forward.

I'm across.

"You did it," says Dad.

I chuck him the rope and we continue down river. All the channels look frozen now, although overflow is still running over top. Ginger picks her feet up carefully, trying to keep them dry, but it's no use, and at least she doesn't refuse to go. Pepper barks and nips at the water. Salt winces with each splash like the water's going to attack him.

Then we're walking on dry snow and it feels easier. Mountains are on both sides of the river still, but farther back from the banks. From now on, even if we find open water again, we'll be able to detour through the trees.

Caribou and wolf tracks are patterned over the ice and the mountainsides. Snow buntings and lapland longspurs are flying overhead in great bunches to nest on the tundra. A bloodthirsty mosquito keeps landing on my cheek.

The next few miles are easy. The river is frozen from bank to bank, and the dogs keep up a steady pace. The cabin is twenty miles from our last camping spot and I can't imagine making it so far tonight, but I remember Mum and Dad saying that I wouldn't be able to carry a litter of pups to town and I know I have to do it. It's easier if I don't think about how tired I am.

The valley by our cabin narrows, so any animals that are following game trails along the river are funneled into a narrow strip of forest between cliffs. It's like an oasis for game. We see more from home than almost anywhere else. But mostly it's wolf and caribou country. There are caribou trails on the mountains that are hundreds of years old, cut deep into the lichen and over the rocks. Dad once said that if it was legal, you could snare caribou on these trails because they can use the same routes year after year, moving up and over the faces of the mountains, single file.

Dad's toboggan gets farther and farther ahead. A few times he stops and waits for me, and Mum kneels down on her snowshoes even farther ahead and waits for him. If Ginger wasn't ready to have her pups, I'd jump on behind the handlebars and let the dogs pull me along. I try to drag my thoughts back to caribou and wolves but they won't go. My eyes keep trying to close.

"What's the problem?" yells Dad.

"I'm tired." I say. Ginger nuzzles my hand and I scratch behind her ears. Pepper whines to go faster. "I can't go any quicker."

Dad looks tired, too. Funny, but over the past few days I've stopped checking his face so often. I didn't realize I was doing it until I quit.

"Want a break?" he asks.

"Okay." I put up my hand in front of Ginger's face. "Stay!" I tell her, making a chopping motion. "Down!" I push down on her back. I've been training her with hand as well as voice signals so if I ever need her to be quiet, like when I take her out hunting, I won't need to talk.

I start up toward Dad. Pepper lunges in his traces and screams to get going, but when I speak sharply to him he sits, howls sadly and then lies down. I perch on top of Dad's toboggan and look around.

Mum comes back and takes out the hot juice and rocket fuel from the bag hanging on the handlebars. It's dusky now. I can only see the shape of trees along the bank and hear owls calling from the darkening forest. It's calm and barely below freezing.

Sitting is even worse than standing. It only makes me want to lie down. It's hours past bedtime. Rachel is breathing loudly in her sleeping bag nest on top of the load with only her face peeking out.

"You're too tired to walk, Becky," Mum says softly.

Her voice seems to be coming from far away. I have

to concentrate to make out the words. I get to my feet and take a few deep breaths.

"I'd like to sleep for awhile," I admit. Since our fight in the tent, she's paid more attention to me. Before she wouldn't have noticed, because she was too busy worrying about Dad.

"Crawl into the sleeping bag," she says. "There's room to sleep in front of Rachel. Ginger will follow behind the other toboggan."

"Ginger," I think, sinking down on the sled bag. For a few minutes I'd almost forgotten about her.

Dad's looking way off in the distance at the mountains. He's checking out the slopes with the binoculars.

"Want to see?" he asks, sticking the glasses in my hands. I focus on a line of white specks pawing away the snow in an alpine bowl. Dall sheep, the wild white sheep that live on the ridge-tops, leap over the broken rocks, beautiful with their curled-back amber horns and their amazing hooves that can suction onto rock.

"No big rams," I say.

"They're not with the ewes this time of year," Dad tells me. "Once they hit about three, the rams stay in their own band for most of the year."

As I watch, a ewe jumps onto a sheer rock face and clings there a moment before leaping on.

"She reminds me of Rachel," I say. I'm so tired that I don't even realize I'm talking out loud until Mum asks to see. I hand her the binoculars and she adjusts them over her own glasses.

Dad seems to be in a good mood. This might be my only chance.

"Dad?" I say. "I've figured out how I can get the puppies to town."

There's no answer. Mum puts down the binoculars and pours herself more hot juice.

"I can pack them to town," I say. "I'm going to sew a special pack that isn't very deep. That way the pups can poke their heads out the top of it."

"How will you keep them in it?" asks Mum.

"I'll sew a belt around the middle."

"The trouble is," says Dad, "that you probably won't be able to do it. You're already tired tonight, aren't you?" This is hard to deny as I'm lying on the sled bag looking up at the faint beginnings of stars. "It will be much harder if you're carrying a pack full of puppies. What if we get halfway out and run out of food because we're taking so long?"

Mum puts her hand on my shoulder and shoves the thermos back in the bag.

"I'll get out a sleeping bag for you," she says. "Tie Ginger's collar to the back of the big toboggan and climb on top of the load. You need some sleep."

I heave myself reluctantly off the sled bag and walk back to Ginger, where she's still lying patiently on the ice waiting for me. Her white tail thumps as I stoop to pat her. I hug the other two dogs tight around their necks.

"No, thanks, Mum," I call over my shoulder. "I'm going to walk."

10

THE NIGHT becomes dream-like after that, very dark with stars not only shining over the river, but filling the depths of space. Looking up is like looking into a forest. Some stars are farther away than others and every so often a star shoots across the dark and disappears. Somewhere beyond the river ice I hear a steady drip of snow melting off rock bluffs and cut-banks.

Then, as the night grows colder, the dripping stops and I hear only the breath of the dogs pulling and the creak of the toboggan and the rub of collars and traces. I no longer need to stop myself from thinking about sleep. It seems like I have been moving along this dark, frozen landscape forever.

Then Dad calls out, "We've come halfway! Ten miles."

Nobody answers. We simply keep walking and the dogs keep pulling.

Sometime in the night, I leave Ginger's side and walk behind my sled, pushing the handlebars to keep the sled on the trail as it curves. Ten miles. I've never walked so far in my life! Surely Ginger can pull for a bit. I can hop on to see how she does.

But then I remember the feel of the puppy wriggling under my fingers...

My legs ache, then stop aching. Later I notice they're hurting again. My calves feel tight, like I've been racing up a cliff.

All I have to do is keep moving and the night will end.

I hear footsteps and then I'm being picked up like Rachel and carried.

"Don't," I say, and Dad puts me down. The stars no longer have depth. The sky is brightening.

"You've proven your point," says Dad. "Don't worry about Ginger. Dogs are tougher than you think. She's just walking along. She's not pulling. I'll keep an eye on her."

"You don't have to. I can walk."

He looks down at me, his face shadowed.

"You're holding us up," he says. "We can make better time if you're not walking." Stiffly, he picks me up and places me on top of the load of the big toboggan. I feel a warm sleeping bag tucked around me and a caribou hide underneath me, and his hand resting for a moment on my head. I almost feel safe and happy.

Then Mum yells, "Let's go!" And the toboggan breaks out and creaks along with me inside it.

My eyes close. I blink to keep them open, and then I

realize I've slept and the sun has sailed over the mountain ridges across the river from the cabin.

I know exactly where we are. We'll be home in a couple of hours. We've walked down this far plenty of times simply to go fishing for the afternoon. It's our backyard. Sunlight spills over the ice until it's sparkling blue and bright as fire. I close my eyes.

•••

Something wet splashes my face. Something so cold it stings.

Water!

I struggle out of my sleeping bag cocoon. The toboggan is out in the river current?

Dad is already on the far bank in front of our cabin. He is pulling on a rope attached to Egypt's harness. My toboggan is already over and my dogs are curled up dozing in their traces. Dad and Mum have taken my team over without me.

Behind me, Rachel starts to cry.

"It's okay," I say. "We're at the cabin. See? The river's just open here. We'll be across in a moment."

"I'm scared," says Rachel. Rachel never says she's scared.

"No problem," I tell her, more water splashing my face. "This toboggan can double as a boat. Besides, the water's shallow."

It's more or less true, and the sled bag is made of a new material that's so waterproof it will keep the load floating. For a while, at least.

Rachel leans her head against my chest. I hear the plop of her thumb going in.

Dad is crouching, leaning back, hauling with his whole weight on Egypt's rope. She doesn't want to swim across. Maybe the current's too strong, because she's drifting downstream with it and we're about to follow in the sled.

"Let's go," yells Mum. She's standing at the back of the toboggan behind us, pushing. "You can do it!"

Egypt is swimming now, but with the current. Dad's getting pulled toward us by her rope.

"Stay where you are," I tell Rachel. "Hang on to Taffy. You're in charge of Taffy." I jump off the load into the river and grab the handlebars beside Mum. Dad's cap has fallen off his head and he's right at the edge of the river.

Mum and I get on the downriver side of the sled and push. Water is breaking against our legs, and it's so cold that it stabs like a burn. The current tears at my thighs, and I stay upright by pushing. I know if I let go, I'll be lost downstream.

But Egypt's turning toward Dad now and behind her, the rest of the team follows. I glance up only long enough to see her head bobbing in the current. She's whining, and Dad crashes backwards still hauling on the rope, and now it's slack and Egypt's no longer swimming. She's walking in the shallows, then shaking herself on shore.

My legs no longer burn. They're numb. The water is smashing against my knees, then calves. Dad is walking backwards pulling on the rope, and the rest of the dogs climb out and shake, one after the other. I hop on the back of the sled and ride the toboggan through the shallows and onto shore. Mum splashes behind me. A dipper is singing somewhere.

I jump off on dry ground. We're home!

The numbness in my legs doesn't last long. Pins and needles start, then stabbing pain. I hop up and down. Rachel chucks out Taffy and vaults off behind her. Warmth spreads through my feet. I stop jumping. Rachel is shedding her snowpants and jacket and mitts and hat.

"What are you doing?" I ask.

"Mud puddling," says Rachel. "I want to try the splits in the mud." She tears off her shirt and sweatpants and tosses them over her shoulder.

The sun fills the clearing around the cabin now, while Rachel laughs, pale in her underwear and boots.

"Come on," she says. "You can practice handstands. It will be soft when you crash."

Mum and Dad are busy with the dogs and taking window shutters off the cabin.

"On your mark, get set, go!" shouts Rachel and races herself into a puddle the size of a house.

Why not? I'm already wet. I run in and out fast, shouting along with Rachel.

"Wait," I say. "I've got to look after my dogs."

But Ginger, Salt and Pepper are curled in balls in their traces. And when I pick up the traces and shake them, there's no response.

I grab jerky from the sled bag and hold it under Pepper's nose. From a sound sleep, he jumps to his feet in a split second, snaps up the jerky and lurches forward, as if he's trying to break out a load. I undo the snap connecting his harness to the traces and wiggle the harness over his legs, chest and neck.

"Easy, boy," I tell him, ruffling the fur on his head. I march him up the trail into the clearing and snap him to a tree. "I'll figure out something for a house for you later." But Pepper doesn't care. Before I finish talking, he's curled up in the snow, tail tucked under his head, sleeping.

Next Salt. I try the same jerky trick but he, of course, doesn't jump to his feet at all. He whines but manages to eat his strip nervously, like it's going to eat him instead.

I try to drag Salt up the trail but he won't walk to the clearing. So I give up and tie him right there. He leans his whole weight against me and rubs his head against my side.

"Stiff, old boy?" I ask him, and he licks my hand. Maybe it smells like jerky, but it's a start.

When I get back, Ginger has both eyes open and is watching for me. I kneel down in the snow beside her and feed her a jerky strip. When she's done, I cradle her head in my lap.

"I'm sorry," I tell her. "I wish you could have been on top of that toboggan last night instead of me."

She answers by talking in her throat and turning up the corners of her mouth in a husky smile. Dad told me that wolves do it sometimes when they're rubbing against their leader.

"Do you want to bring her inside?"

I look up. Mum's standing beside me.

"Come on, girl," she croons to Ginger. Ginger perks up her ears and slowly stands, shaking the last drops of river water from her white fur.

"She should be comfortable," says Mum. "I'll make her a bed inside when I've got everything unpacked."

"I'll make her a bed," I say. And I lead Ginger up the trail and into the cabin.

The cabin is exactly like it was when we left it. For a moment I don't remember everything that's gone wrong since then, how Dad's brain has got sick and Mum has wanted the family to split up. I don't remember that Dad and Mum don't want to take Ginger's pups back to town, that I haven't actually figured out how I can do it.

I stand in the doorway, and the memories of so many happy times here sweep over me.

I take one last look around the cabin before heading to town. Most of our belongings are safely boxed in the cache — a little treehouse with tin wrapped around each supporting tree to keep animals from climbing up — and the cabin doesn't look the same. I feel Dad's arm around me. Mum's whistling somewhere outside.

"I'm going to harness the dogs," says Dad. "Want to give me a hand?"

"I don't want to leave," I tell him.

"We'll be back, Becky," he says. "We'll always be back."

The cabin is simple, built of notched logs and chinked with moss Rachel and I picked in the forest around the clearing. When you come in there's a long room that's a kitchen and kind of living room. At the end to the left is Mum and Dad's bedroom. At the end to the right is mine and Rachel's. A bookcase divides our room into our own areas.

I lead Ginger behind the door.

"Don't you think she should be over by the stove?" asks Mum. "The cabin's cool because the shutters have been on the windows."

"Okay." Sunlight is bathing the worn floorboards. It's the first sun these rooms have felt since we were last here. Log walls take a couple of days to warm up before they hold the heat of the rooms.

Rachel is out in the clearing yelling as she splashes in the puddle.

"Look, look," she shouts. "I'm doing the splits. I'm doing it!"

I hear a tremendous splash.

"Mum!" yells Rachel. "I'm soaked."

I put my arm around Ginger's neck and laugh.

Mum peers out the window and laughs herself.

"Now that would make a good picture," she says. "Rachel in the puddle in her underwear and boots and the snow and mountains as the backdrop." Her hand reaches behind her ear where she used to keep her pencil.

"There's chores to do," Dad reminds me. "There's the toboggan to unload and wood to bring in. Make sure Rachel gives you a hand."

He should have seen Mum reaching for her pencil. I bet he hasn't even noticed that she's not getting her sketches done. Or that Rachel's sitting in a mud puddle, not exactly dressed for chores.

Sighing, Ginger makes herself comfortable beside the already lit stove. She sticks her nose in my hand and rubs it against me.

"Rachel can bring in the wood by herself for once," says Mum. "As soon as she finds something dry to wear."

She sighs and looks at Dad.

"You can unpack the sled," she tells him. "Becky and I have got spruce boughs to gather. This dog needs a decent bed."

11

MUM AND I punch through the snow crust in the woods, gathering spruce boughs for Ginger. Snow reflects the sunlight, making my eyes squint from the glare. The sun is over the mountains and very hot and the snow is melting by the moment around the spruce trees and along the riverbank. There's a carpet of wizened leaves and moss on the cut-banks, the first place to show bare earth. The dirt looks very black beside the snow.

Ice cracks like a gunshot, then settles, cracks booming from bank to bank as they spread. The river is flowing now. Overflow has seeped up through the cracks from the current below the ice and is spreading along the river's surface.

"Good thing we're here," says Mum. "I wouldn't want to be wading through that water out there now."

"Me either. Or the dogs. Not without Bear to lead them." I wait for a moment, hoping she'll answer. Nobody in the family has mentioned Bear's dying. The heart has gone out of Dad's team, and we're all supposed to pretend that things are just the same.

Mum is looking out over the ice with a faraway look on her face that she gets when she's about to have a carving idea. I've seen it all my life. We'll be walking along talking or just doing something together and then I'll see that she's staring hard and not moving.

When we get back to the cabin after one of these times, she takes out her paper and draws what she's been looking at. Later that night from my bed, I'll see her hunched over in her chair, her arm crooked to hold the knife in a pool of lamplight, shaping the block of wood. When she is done, though, her face is so happy that I like to be near her. The happy feeling seems to spill out of her.

I've missed that this year, the feeling I get from Mum when she's carving. I've missed Mum.

Usually I love it when Mum is getting a carving idea. But not now.

"Mum? We need to talk about the puppies."

"Now?"

"Dad said last night that I've proven myself. So I can pack Ginger's pups to town, can't I? It's obvious we're not going to be running dogs."

"You've proven that you're willing to try hard." Her face is losing that I've-got-a-carving-idea look, fast as a pricked balloon. "But I still don't think you can do it. You'll try until you make yourself sick like you almost did last night, but you won't be able to get them there." She looks sad again.

"All you and Dad have to do is let me try."

"Becky. I want you to have a puppy. I probably want it as much as you do. But I'm not making promises that I can't keep."

"Even if Dad says no, you have to let me try." Mum and Dad have always backed each other up.

"If I think it's the right thing to do," says Mum, after a long pause, "then I'll say so. Don't worry about Dad's moods affecting anything."

"What's wrong with him really?" I ask. "He's not even nice to you sometimes."

"I don't know what's happened to him." Mum holds out her hand for me to take. "But each of us has our own dreams. We'll still have them whether Dad gets better or not."

I think about that. Maybe it's true, but I still don't want to be without Dad.

"Do we have to live without Dad?" I ask.

"I can't answer that yet." She hugs me close against her red plaid coat.

A golden immature eagle across the river is rising on a wind. He's soaring on a draft over the mountain peaks, now circling with tilted wings. The sun on my face is hot and the smell of forest drifts over the clearing.

The eagle begins to soar in tighter and tighter circles, catching a downdraft, then rising farther up. It is very beautiful against the blue spring sky and the sound of the settling ice. Every so often melting snow crashes from a tree and the tree seems to stand a little straighter and taller.

All my life I'll remember this spring, coming home with the snow melting and the river almost breaking under our feet.

"The older I get," Mum says, "the less I'm sure of. The more I look at something that I'm going to carve, the less I know about it. Dad's being sick has felt like that for me."

A little brown dipper is hopping over the open channel, trilling its spring song. Every so often he stops, hops off his stone perch and dives into the current for a snack.

Mum watches the dipper for so long that I think she's finished.

"I wonder sometimes if things have happened in Dad's life that I know nothing about," she says finally. "Maybe those things have made him depressed, too, not just chemicals. But I do know one thing. Whatever caused the darkness to go inside him, it's our job to not let it into us."

Can darkness really spread from person to person?

The dipper's song moves up and down the scale, like violin notes. Another brown scrap of bird glides over the cracking ice and lands, tiny claws outstretched. They stand side by side and sing, bobbing their heads.

Mum breaks an armful of boughs off a nearby spruce tree and hands them to me.

"We're getting spruce boughs for Ginger. Remember?"

Suddenly we hear Dad's voice calling from the cabin across the clearing.

"Becky! Come here quickly!"

Whatever he wants, it sounds important. I take the last boughs from Mum's arms and run back along the trail.

•••

When my eyes adjust to the light inside the cabin, I see Dad standing by the kitchen stove, looking thin, pinched and old in a gray shirt and baggy wool pants. Beside him, Ginger is digging at the floorboards.

I drop the spruce boughs and push her down onto them.

"Sit, Ginger," I say. She looks in my face and whimpers. I throw my arms around her neck. "It's okay, old girl. It's going to be okay."

"Becky," says Dad.

"Yes."

"She probably needs some water."

The door creaks shut behind Mum. She places her spruce boughs beside Ginger, who collapses onto her side, whining again.

"Is Ginger having her puppies?" Rachel asks.

"Yes," says Mum, putting her hand on my shoulder.

Ginger cries out again, and something falls from between her legs. A wet, wiggling bundle is moving inside something that looks like a bloody plastic bag. Ginger turns back as if to bite at herself. She whimpers and shuffles and sniffs at the bag. Then she licks at it hard, tearing the sac. I hear squealing as she licks even harder.

"Ginger," I breathe, and she wags her tail and raises her head, and instead of a wet bundle scrunched tight in a bag, I see a puppy squirming on the floor.

I pick up the warm, wet pup and lay it carefully on the spruce bough bed.

"Here, Ginger," I coax, and this time she nuzzles the puppy so it fits right into her side. It's colored exactly like her, white all over, but so skinny that its sides look collapsed. It squeaks again, and then doesn't.

For a long minute, we all watch. How can that be a life — a few squeals on a kitchen floor? Mum picks up the pup and cradles it in the palm of her hand. It doesn't move. Mum presses her fingers gently against the pup's stomach.

"Sorry, Becky," she says. "This one's dead."

Rachel burst into sobs. "That's not fair," she shouts and dashes into our bedroom.

Mum looks from me to the bedroom door. "I have to go talk to her," she says. "I'll be right back."

Crouching beside Ginger, I nod and cradle her head. I want someone to comfort me.

"I'll get rid of the puppy," says Dad, standing over me.

"No. Leave it. I'll bury it properly later."

I can see that there are tears in his eyes.

"What's wrong with you?" I ask. "You don't want any pups anyhow. You can quit worrying how to get this one back to town now."

Dad doesn't answer. He takes the little white puppy and disappears outside with it.

"Leave it on my sled bag for me," I yell after him. "I'll take care of it."

I'm going to bury it and mark the spot so I can always find it. One day when Ginger is old, I'll bury her beside the puppy. I want to remember it. I don't want it to be like it never existed.

After a long time, I feel Mum's hand on my shoulder. I realize she's been calling me.

"Becky," she says. "I'm sorry, but Dad and I have to get wood."

I look up. "Now? Can't you wait?" I never talk like this, but I don't want to be by myself.

"Now," says Mum. "I'm so sorry, but we'll be right back. I'd wait, but our dry wood is piled just across the creek. The ice is going much earlier than we'd planned. Even tonight may be too late."

I hear Mum and Dad leaving — pulling the toboggan

themselves because the dogs are too exhausted. Rachel is still in the bedroom. I should be watching her but I can't bring myself to move. Ginger's sides are no longer heaving. She doesn't look pregnant anymore at all. But she keeps licking me, and the feel of her warmth is all that keeps me from running away. At some point, I bury my face in her fur and cry. Once I start, I can't stop.

I thought that Dad would help me train them — who can resist puppies? I thought he would remember how we used to be partners with his dogs and be proud that I was working with my own team.

Finally, there are no tears left in me to come out.

When I look up, Rachel is kneeling on the floor.

"Becky," she says. "There's another one. Look."

I kneel beside Rachel and place my hand very softly on Ginger's belly. Something thin and hard twitches under my fingers. A puppy's leg! Ginger breathes more quickly and her sides begin to heave. She stops, then heaves again, over and over.

"You're right," I say.

"Is it having a hard time being born?" Rachel.

"I only saw pups being born once," I tell her. "When Dad's friend's dog had puppies."

Ginger begins to pant. She turns her head and tries to bite at something between her legs.

"Easy, girl," I say. I take my hand away from her stomach and stroke her head.

Ginger's pants grow closer together, slow, then

quicken again, over and over. Nothing happens. No puppy is born. Rachel sits very still patting Ginger's head. Salt whimpers from the clearing.

"This pup needs to come out soon," I say. My hand is still on her stomach. "The pups I watched had no problem being born but the musher told me what to do if they took too long." He also said what would happen if they took too long coming out, but I'm not going to mention that.

"Can we help her?"

"The pup should come out by itself. But if it doesn't come soon, we could try giving it a hand, maybe turning it a bit… inside."

Rachel rubs her hands down Ginger's spine. Ginger lays her head back on the spruce boughs and whimpers.

"It's okay, girl," I say, over and over.

What a stupid thing to say. How do I know it's going to be okay? And how do I know that I won't hurt her more by trying to help her? What if she dies like Bear? Then it won't matter if she trusts me or not.

"I'm here, girl," I whisper. "I'll take care of you. I'll stay with you."

After a long time like this with Rachel stroking Ginger and me whispering to her, Rachel gets up and pours me hot tea. She even puts in sugar, just the way I love it, real hot and sweet.

"Thanks," I say. Rachel kneels down again and we pass the cup back and forth.

I pour a few drops of tea onto a saucer and put it under Ginger's nose. She raises her head, sniffs and laps it up. I give her more and more and then Rachel, without saying a word, gets up and refills the mug.

Ginger whimpers again. The sound is getting quieter, like she is wearing out. She lies down, gets up, over and over. She can't get comfortable.

The tea has cooled. I glance out the window and realize hours have gone by. Mum and Dad should have been home long ago. I light a lamp, and it throws shadows over Rachel's face.

"I don't think this pup is going to make it," I tell her.

12

I'M TIRED, even more tired than I was walking on the river ice last night. I want somebody to take charge, but I know that isn't going to happen.

"I'm going to do it," I say. "I'm going to feel and see if the pup needs some help."

"You don't know how. Maybe you'll hurt Ginger more."

"It's okay," I say. Rachel needs me to be the grown-up. She needs to think I can take care of things. "Ginger's already in pain. She and the puppy deserve a chance to live."

Rachel shrugs and looks away, tears trickling down her cheeks.

"I'll need your help, you know," I tell her.

She rubs the tears away with her fists.

"Okay," she says, taking a deep breath.

"Put your arm around Ginger's neck like you're going to pat her — not like you're holding her down. But I need you to keep her very still."

Ginger is almost too tired to whimper now. I can see each contraction clearly against the stillness of her body. Without stopping to think, I reach between her legs. Part of me wants to run to where Mum and Dad are loading firewood and part of me knows that even Mum's hand would be too big. Slowly, I press between Ginger's legs and up through the birth canal.

Then I stop. Ginger is whining in the back of her throat like she's talking to me, like she knows I'm trying to help her. I hear Rachel murmuring but I can't make out the words.

I'm lying on the floor and it's hard to see more than outlines in the dim cabin even with the lamp lit. I close my eyes. It's a trick Mum taught me from when she's stuck on a carving. She said that if she closes her eyes, her mind is able to focus better.

When I shut my eyes, I can feel the pup. It's hard, solid. I tighten my fingers and the solid thing moves.

The pup is alive! I squeeze it with my fingers, and it squirms against them.

"I've got it," I say, grinning at Rachel over the rise of Ginger's chest.

Slowly, I wriggle my hand. I can feel around the squirming pup now. It feels jammed tight. I try to shift it.

There's no movement. No wonder Ginger isn't able to get this pup out. She makes the throat-talking sound again but this time the sound is shriller and softer at the same time. Finally, she moans and is silent.

"Can't you hurry?"

I grab what I can reach of the pup with my hand and turn it like a doorknob. Nothing. I turn it in the opposite direction. This time there's a little movement, like a jam jar lid that's about to come loose.

For a moment I pause, opening my eyes. Rachel has moved the lamp beside me on the floor. But I don't want to see. It's like my fingers have become my eyes. And the puppy and my fingers can almost feel together.

The sled scrapes in the clearing. Logs thud as Mum and Dad throw them onto the ground.

"This little guy is going to be my wheel dog," I say out loud. The wheel dog's usually the strongest dog, who can keep the toboggan straight no matter how rough the trail.

The door swings open.

"I'm so sorry," begins Mum. "The creek wasn't safe. We had to build a bridge."

At that moment, the pup begins to slip down.

"He's coming!" I shout.

I rest my arm a moment. This time the pup seems to be moving by himself. I feel him slipping down and I know he's free.

He can come now.

I take out my hand. There's blood on it but I don't care. I sit back on my heels.

"You can let go of Ginger now," I say.

Rachel scoots over beside me. The lamplight throws

shadows over Ginger's white fur, and she turns her head and whines once. Mum kneels down beside us. All I can see of Dad are his boots.

There on the spruce boughs is another clear bag of puppy. Ginger licks away the birth sac. I can't see the pup for her head.

"This puppy's coming with us, Dad," I tell him.

Across the clearing, the ice cracks and cracks again. I hear the boom as the cracks spread from bank to bank under the puddled overflow.

I hear a whimper from under Ginger's tongue. She has finished licking her pup and is eating something that looks like liver.

"Becky?" asks Rachel.

"Yes?"

"Is this one going to live?"

"Sure thing," I tell her. "Listen to him."

The puppy is wriggling and squeaking on the boughs. Rachel peers closer.

"A boy," she says.

Dad puts his hand on my arm.

"Look at him," he says.

I lift the pup and hold him in the lamplight.

He's huge! I feel that as soon as I hold him. He's solid-ly round —no, fat — with an enormous head and floppy ears. I have to cup my hands tightly. I hold him so the light shines over him.

He's still wet. He doesn't look a bit like Ginger,

though. He looks like — and then I see what Dad means — like a Newfoundland and Irish setter cross.

I rub my fingers along his back to dry it and check the fur. The last time I felt this pup he was inside Ginger. It seems too incredible to be true.

His fur is black. I dry his tail and fluff it out by rubbing backwards with my fingers. There are red plumes on his tail. His chest is massive and his legs are long.

"Do you see?" asks Mum.

I nod, my throat tight.

"He's Bear's pup." I rub along his legs and stomach and finally his neck. "But he's like Ginger, too." Starting at his neck and spreading over his chest is a patch of white fur.

The pup squeaks. He squeaks louder and louder — how can a newborn make so much noise? — and wriggles in my hands until I place him gently at Ginger's side. She thumps her tail.

The puppy struggles forward, searching with his nose until he finds a nipple and latches on. Behind me I hear Mum carrying Rachel off to bed.

Has the whole day really gone by?

"I'm not tired," she protests.

"Just a nap," says Mum.

Dad and I sit watching Ginger and Bear's pup while the northern lights dance outside the kitchen window. Logs settle in the stove, and Dad pours us both hot tea.

I know that no other pups will be born. It's okay,

though. In fact, it's better because I won't have a litter to take back to town. One little pup can snuggle in my backpack and not cause any problems at all.

I've dreamed of a line of dogs with the long legs of the new racing dogs and the deep chests of the old-timers' freighting dogs. Bear's puppy will be the start of my line.

I've already taken a team of culls that other mushers thought were only good to shoot and I've turned them into workers, into a team of my own with heart. What can I do with a dog like this special pup?

"Remember, Dad, how you always told me I could breed my own line of dogs? Now I'm doing it."

"I knew you would, Becky," he says.

I reach over and stroke the pup's warm back. He has finished nursing and has fallen asleep with his mouth open. Every so often he burps, twitches and relaxes again. His fur is dry and fluffy. In the lamplight, I see the black back, the red-plumed setter tail and the white chest like his mother. I feel like I've known him my whole life.

I fall asleep beside Ginger and the pup. At some point, I wake to find I'm lying by the cook stove with Ginger breathing in my ear. Someone has thrown a sleeping bag over me and placed a pillow under my head. I reach over to pat Ginger and notice Dad at the kitchen table drinking tea.

"Go back to sleep, Becky," he says. Then I see Mum

walking out of their bedroom carrying a lamp in one hand.

"Are you okay, Becky?" she asks me. "Aren't you going to bed?"

"I need to keep an eye on Ginger and the pup," I say sleepily.

"Okay," says Mum. "Just don't get cold."

"I need to talk to you," Dad tells her.

Mum simply stands in the doorway holding the lamp, and its shadows light up her face so it looks soft and young. Her hair is hanging loose over her shoulders.

Then she turns back into their room. Dad gets up and follows her, and I see the wedge of light shrinking as the door closes behind him.

Beside Ginger, the pup stretches and yawns and snuggles in close again to nurse.

Chili, I think, is the bounciest spice of all. His name is Chili.

13

I WAKE UP often during the night to reach over and check that Ginger and the pup are all right. For a while I hear Mum and Dad murmuring in the dark, though I can't make out the actual words. Chili makes a lot of noise for someone only a few hours old!

Finally it's morning, and Rachel is throwing herself across the room doing handstands. She hovers upright, flops over into a ball and springs up beside me.

"How's the puppy?" she asks, kneeling beside him.

"He's doing great — already fatter."

I scoop him up and hold him out to her. His belly is hard and round. He squirms and squeaks.

"Chili," I say, "meet Rachel."

Rachel cuddles the little guy against her chest. He moves his head back and forth, looking for milk.

"Ouch," she says. "He's sucking on my shirt. Gross!" She hands him back to me like he's hot, and I tuck him in beside Ginger.

"Pancakes anyone?" asks Mum. She's standing by the

table with her shirt untucked and her hair tousled and her feet bare. There's a pencil stuck behind her ear. She yawns and stretches. "I'm hungry," she says, rubbing her eyes.

"I want ten pancakes," says Rachel, flipping backwards. "And a whole river of syrup." She jumps up, clicks her legs together like scissors and leaps into another handstand. Her legs hit a shelf and piles of paperbacks rain onto her head. It doesn't slow her down, though. She folds herself into a ball and forward rolls toward the opposite wall.

"Yes!" she says, jumping to her feet.

We all laugh. Dad is standing in the bedroom doorway watching. He only smiles with the corners of his mouth, but at least he's making an effort.

Only a day ago we were mushing through the night trying to beat the overflow back to the cabin. Now we're home and laughing, and instead of a lead dog pregnant with a litter of pups that I don't know what I'll do with, I have one monster puppy who's going to be mine all his life.

But there's one last thing I have to do. I pull on my boots and jacket.

"I'll be back soon," I tell them. "Keep an eye on Chili and Ginger for me."

The morning air is crisp and the sky is deep blue with a few wisps of cloud snapping across it. I can see the trail we broke through the night, the toboggan tracks across the clearing, down the bank and then lost under a couple of feet of overflow.

We'll never be able to return on our back trail now — too much water flowing over the ice. We'll have to wait until the ground is dry and then cut overland across the passes on foot.

I walk along the bank, and the sun rises over the mountains and washes the snow with light. The snow is firm on the surface from last night's frost. Under the crust, though, is slush. The ground beneath the spruce trees is bare moss and black earth. Sunshine spills over the moss.

Then I see them. Small, oval green leaves with red berries splashed among them.

Lowbush cranberries, fresh after their winter sleep under the snow! I take off my hat, kneel and pick.

Every plant that I pick from has green leaves — not withered or dry but leaves as moist as when the snow first fell. The berries smell yeasty, like Mum's bread when it's rising. I wander from tree to tree and search in the moss until the bottom of my hat is covered.

Later, I'll bring the white puppy here and place him beneath the broadest tree. I'll cover him with the prettiest rocks I can find, and before I say goodbye, I'll give him a name. Not a spice name like my other dogs but something sweet.

Sugar, I'll call him Sugar.

All around me the snow-crust is melting. A warm breeze is moving the tops of the spruce trees.

Chili. I say my pup's name out loud. In twelve days his eyes will be open and he'll be able to recognize me. In three weeks he can follow me around outside. In a month, if we're still at the cabin, he'll be snuffling through the new grass and learning to come when I call him.

A raven is flying from our bank to the far one. It tilts and glides on black wings, calling and wheeling back.

I put down my hat and go over to a bare bit of ground. I plant my legs carefully apart and leap onto my hands. Then I walk on them, teetering, until they brush against snow. I spring to my feet.

"Yes!" I shout.

Suddenly, the river ice cracks like a pistol shot. Under the near bank where the current runs quickest, a layer of ice drops. A river otter pokes his head up and twitches his whiskers. He looks like a puppy.

I want everyone to see him.

"Come here!" I shout, racing toward the cabin, my berry-filled hat bouncing. "There's an otter in the open channel."

The otter scrambles out of the water and slides through the overflow and up the bank. He pauses at the top, wriggles his whiskers again and slides down what looks like a toboggan's trough — his trail.

Dad is standing in the sunshine, his face covered with shaving soap, a cigarette dangling from his mouth. Mum comes out with Rachel at her side and her sketch-pad in one hand. We stroll together down to the river-bank. Dad kneels on the bank and splashes cold water over his face to rinse away the lather. Mum takes the pencil from behind her ear.

When Dad stands again, his gray beard is gone and I see his thin face clearly like I haven't done for a long time. Rachel springs wildly down the bank on her hands, and the otter vanishes.

Mum grins and puts her arm with the pencil around my shoulder. On the open page of her sketchbook I can see the outlines of our cabin kitchen and Ginger. I think I can see me kneeling beside her.

"It's spring," says Mum.

Pepper begins to howl happily from the clearing. Salt joins in, then Dad's dogs. Cabin smoke drifts toward the sunlit peaks.

I take a deep breath of mountain air. We're home.

JOANNE BELL was born in England and is a graduate of the MFA program in creative writing at the University of British Columbia. She spent ten years traveling by dog team and living in remote cabins in Yukon's Ogilvie Mountains — an experience that inspired this, her first novel. Joanne lives in Dawson City, Yukon Territory, where she works as a teacher and literacy tutor.